TOUGH MESSES

WATERVALE
PUBLISHING

Books by R.M. Lowery

Laytons Grove
What Was Left
When Kristen Comes Home

—

The Jakob Larsen Mysteries
The Gentle Slope
We Kill Our Own
Time Fades Away

TOUGH MESSES

Eleven Stories of Crime and Desperation

R.M. LOWERY

WATERVALE PUBLISHING

WATERVALE PUBLISHING

First published in the United States of America

Copyright © 2025 by R.M. Lowery

First Edition: August 2025

"Luxury Goods" first published in *Black Cat Mystery Magazine*, August 2024; "Good Neighbors" first published in an R.M. Lowery newsletter, March 2022; and "The Road Out" first published in *The First Line*, Winter 2024.

Cover photo by Tobias Kleeb
Cover & interior design by Watervale Publishing

ISBN-13: 979-8-9933962-0-0

For Huxley, forever my buddy.

CONTENTS

Moving Day ❖ 1

Luxury Goods ❖ 15

Flush ❖ 34

Leaky Pipe ❖ 51

I Like You, You Seem Nice ❖ 64

Tough Messes ❖ 76

Sicko ❖ 91

Good Neighbors ❖ 109

Quality Time ❖ 120

Bankrupt ❖ 138

The Road Out ❖ 156

Acknowledgments ❖ 173

TOUGH MESSES

MOVING DAY

Lawns on Sibley Lane are mowed every Monday. Trash and recycling are picked up each Tuesday. HOA dues cover both, and those in charge of the Oxbow Estates HOA always update residents about any deviation from the ordinary. So, understandably, folks noticed when me and my guys arrived unannounced on a Friday morning and began breaking up concrete.

After we made a couple cuts into the sidewalk with a loud saw, we broke up a small section of concrete and pretended to inspect some underground piping. It gained the attention of a few neighbors, and that's when I sent Big Vince to bang on the Zekman's door.

Dressed in a blue work shirt with a Consumers Energy patch above one pocket and the name DAVE stitched above the other, he rapped on the screen door a couple times before ringing the bell.

I stood at the end of the walkway and watched as Mrs. Zekman answered the door wearing sweatpants and an oversized Red Wings shirt, and though annoyed by the intrusion, she was plenty eager to leave her home once Dave told her that someone reported a gas leak in the area—told her that due to the possibility of a deadly explosion, she and her family needed to evacuate the house immediately.

Her husband, she explained, was out of town on business and wouldn't be home until evening. Her teenage son and daughter were at school. With her out of the house, the place was ours.

A similar scene repeated next door where Johnny, dressed in a uniform bearing the name RICK, got the Holtons out of their home.

On the other side of the Zekman's house, I rang the doorbell of a widow who came to the door with the aid of a walker, the old aluminum kind with tennis balls covering the feet. She was older than me, but not by a lot.

"Yes?" she said, her voice weak and scratchy.

"Hi, Mrs. Colosimo?"

"Yes. How can I help you?"

"I'm terribly sorry to bother you, ma'am, but I'm with the utility company. We've received reports that there might be a gas leak at the home next door. We don't believe that you're in any danger, but out of an abundance of caution, we'd like you to exit your home."

She looked down the street at our truck and the backhoe strapped to the flatbed trailer behind it, then she noticed that many of her neighbors were milling around outside their homes. I could tell she was buying what we were selling. Her face full of concern, she agreed and joined her neighbors on the sidewalk.

We didn't necessarily need the Holtons or Mrs. Colosimo out of their homes, but we needed to be convincing. It was best to get all the neighbors who were at home as involved as possible, so they felt informed, felt like they were a part of the whole thing. And to make sure none of them placed a call to the real gas company. To accomplish all of that, we needed to put on a good show, distract everyone, keep them from realizing that all of this was total bullshit.

Stitched onto my uniform was a patch bearing the name JIMMY, a bit of an inside joke. I chose the name at the last minute as we threw the whole thing together. And that's the thing. We didn't have much time to plan. It was almost five on Thursday when we got word from our guy over at the building department that Todd and Beth Zekman had received a permit to install an in-ground pool in their friggin' basement. Work was to begin Monday.

Now normally, I wouldn't give a fat rat's ass if someone wanted to dig up their basement and blow their hard-earned cash on something as stupid as an indoor swimming pool. Build yourself a wine cellar if you want. Install a damn helipad on the roof for all I care. What you spend your money on is your business, unless you're the Zekmans and you live at 3237 Sibley Lane in West Bloomfield, Michigan.

In the Zekmans' case, I was very much concerned about their home improvement projects, especially when one of those projects involved digging up the foundation. The last goddamned thing I needed was some contractor finding what me and my guys buried beneath that house all those years ago.

We managed to get all our gear in the house and down to the Zekmans' basement on our own. All of us were winded though—fading versions of the young men we were the last time all three of us were together at that spot.

We were prepared for the possibility of a day like this. We had the tools we'd need ready, and a rough plan of attack in place. Although, by the time we'd reached a certain age, we'd gotten complacent, incorrectly assuming the day would never come.

Thankfully the residents of Oxbow Estates were the types of people who respected authority—or at least respected men with hardhats, safety vests, and blue work shirts. Even the kind with patches hastily sewn onto them.

They were also welcoming of one another. Upon seeing a gathering of fellow neighbors at the curb, the woman across the street from the Zekmans popped the cork on a bottle of wine and invited her neighbors in for a little day drinking. Though she rudely neglected to offer us any, I digress. Point is, it was keeping them occupied and that was good because it was anyone's guess how long the job would take us, and if just one of them got clever and called the utility company to verify our story, we'd be screwed.

Finding the body was our only goal, but hell if I remembered where it was buried. Back in the mid-seventies, the neighborhood was nothing but rolling hills of dirt where homes were just beginning to be built, and the area looked nothing like it does these days. Plus, as much as I hated to admit it, I was getting old. I barely remembered what I'd done this week, never mind all the crazy shit we'd done way back when.

We definitely put him under the Zekmans' house though—somewhere under the basement, somewhere in the northeast corner of the sprawling 3,500-square-foot home. It didn't belong to the Zekmans back then though. The house was under construction and was owned by the builder. Someone struck a deal with a guy on one of the construction crews to ignore that we'd dropped the body in a hole on the property—a shallow hole that the guy soon covered in concrete. That guy was later placed in a different hole, but that's another story for another time. Point is, with him gone, only me and the guys knew where the body was, and we planned on keeping it that way.

The last time I saw the place was at the end of July 1975, the day before the basement floor was poured, covering the body of someone who was about to go missing for good. At least that was the plan. And the plan had worked for years, until the goddamned Zekmans decided their bratty children needed a swimming pool.

The Zekmans' basement was finished with wall-to-wall carpeting, and it had good-sized windows, at least for a basement. In the main living area, they had a huge television that sat on an equally huge entertainment center. On the walls, framing the television, were Warhol-style portraits of each kid. Creepy stuff, frankly.

The other side of the basement was what we'd come for. The Zekmans had cleared out the area—removed all the furniture and pulled up the carpeting. It was the spot that, first thing next week, crews would start transforming into the family's new swimming pool.

Vince had grown impatient with my tour of the Zekmans' home and fired up the gas engine of the saw—a deafening sound that reverberated against the solid basement walls. Dropping the diamond blade into the bare concrete floor, he cut a long line near the corner of the basement. The Zekmans had clearly called 811 and had folks come out and mark off where the underground pipes were. The markings helped us know where we shouldn't dig, but didn't exactly tell us where the body was.

I tapped Vince on the shoulder to get his attention. He was annoyed, but the blade was heating up and needed a break anyway. He pushed his safety goggles up to his forehead with a grunt and said, "What?"

"We just gonna cut a bunch of friggin' holes in the ground until we get lucky?"

"You got a better way of finding needles in haystacks?"

He had a point, so I shrugged and let him get back to it. Like I said, I couldn't remember much about those crazy days. Somehow, I lived through them, something few guys can say. Me, Big Vince, and Johnny were the last of that bunch. The last to know the truth.

I wish I had a better memory of everything though. It would have saved us lots of time in the Zekmans' basement. What I do remember about that summer day in '75 was the boss telling me to get my guys together and to be ready when the phone rang. In this thing of ours, when the boss gives an order, you don't ask questions.

The boss had us doing whatever Tony Pro wanted. Tony Pro was a big shot with the Genovese family. He was calling the shots from New Jersey, and he was the one who decided that time was up for Mr. Hoffa. Yeah, *that* Mr. Hoffa.

So Tony Pro set some stuff up—arranged for someone to head to the Red Fox restaurant and pick up Mr. H. I don't remember if I knew that at the time or not. Might've been something I learned later, you know, from the papers and whatnot. It was talked about a lot because it was the last time anyone saw ol' Mr. H. Anyone other than me and my guys, that is.

The disappearing act we helped arrange fueled all kinds of theories. Some folks say that, after being killed in Detroit, his body was shoved into a 55-gallon drum and shipped back to New Jersey so Tony Pro could verify he was dead. Others think his body was sunk in the Atlantic Ocean. Many others say he was dumped at Central Sanitation. There's even a prominent theory that his body is buried under a massive sports complex in New Jersey, one that's home to the Jets and Giants. No one ever mentions Sibley Lane though, which means the boss was right to trust us with this one.

Vince had scored three squares in the floor that were big enough for us to start digging. But before we could start, we'd have to break up some concrete with sledgehammers, and that's what we were about to do when I noticed that

Mrs. Zekman had wandered away from her neighbor's house to check on our progress.

So while Vince finish the last of his cuts, "Rick" and me went outside to have a chat with Mrs. Zekman, to give her an update on how we'd traced the leak to an underground pipe, and to let them know that "Dave" was in the basement trying to isolate and seal the leak.

Mrs. Zekman had a lot of questions though.

She chewed her lip nervously. "Is the gas shut off?"

I nodded as I pretended to read something on my clipboard. "Yes, ma'am. We had to shut it off in order to do the repair work, but we'll have it back on in no time."

"Well, since the gas is off, can I go back inside?"

"I'm sorry, but it's policy that only Consumers Energy personnel can be in a home while performing this kind of work." I scribbled on my clipboard for show. "I do apologize for the inconvenience. We'll have you back inside as soon as we can."

"Couldn't I go in just long enough to get a few items? Some paperwork, maybe some photos? Those things are irreplaceable."

"Sorry, ma'am. Again, that'd be against policy. But like I said, we've shut off the gas to your home, so there's very little risk of anything happening to your photos."

"I don't understand. Why can't I go inside then? I'll be real quick."

Nodding my chin toward Johnny, I said, "Could you head back in and see if Dave needs any help?"

He agreed and headed toward the house. I figured Vince would need help breaking up the concrete, and when it came to swinging a sledgehammer, it was better them than me.

I looked at Mrs. Zekman and said, "I understand your frustration, ma'am. It's my job to enforce policy though. I could get fired if I allow you in, even for a minute or two."

I was talking a lot, but I figured it was best to keep her occupied, best to distract her from questioning any of this too much. I also figured we were close to finding Mr. H, which put us that much closer to packing him up and moving him to his new home.

Vince and Johnny had the three sections of concrete broken up by the time I freed myself from Mrs. Zekman. When I returned to the basement, they were busy digging in the dirt, and when Johnny noticed me standing there, he stopped his work, grabbed a small shovel, and tossed it my way. It landed with a clink, then slid to the toes of my work boots.

Johnny glared at me. "Hey, Gino. Glad you could finally join us, ya chooch."

"Look, someone's gotta keep the locals calm."

"Yeah? And what? We're just s'posed to do all the hard labor while you're out there flapping your lips?"

"Look, asshole. That shit takes finesse, which you don't have."

"So I should be down here, putting my strong back and weak mind to work then, eh?"

Big Vince whistled, a horrible noise more deafening than the saw. "Would both of youse shut the fuck up and dig?"

My initial urge was to pick up the shovel and plant the flat end of it against Vince's thick head. Remind him who's in charge of the crew. But he had a point. We were there for a reason, and we needed to speed things up so we could get the hell out of there while we were able to do it on our own, and not in the back of a police car. So, I drove the shovel into the dirt instead of Vince's skull.

Digging in that spot transported me back to the night we dug Mr. H his home. I had no idea what we were on call for that night. I had no idea that we'd be disposing of one of the most recognizable figures in all of America, but back then, I was in no position to ask questions. So, I did as I was told and got my guys together. We waited at my place, drank some beers, threw some darts. The Tigers were playing the Yankees later that night and I'd hoped to tune into the game, but the phone rang well before the first pitch was thrown. I had a short conversation with someone I didn't know. They gave me an address out in what was, at the time, beyond the outskirts of Detroit. Said the boss wanted me and my guys to drive out there—to some intersection that I doubt I could find today—to meet some other guys in a red Mercury.

We grabbed some pops and cigarettes from a store, then drove out to the spot and parked. The sun set, and we waited. We got out of the car and waited some more. We smoked, and we waited. Finally, the red Mercury crept toward us. Behind it was a black Lincoln.

Two guys got out of the Mercury. One of 'em went straight to the Lincoln and climbed into the back seat. The other, a slender guy, walked over to me. I didn't know him. Someone said both of them were from New Jersey. Again, I don't know if I knew that at the time, or if it's something I heard later. Point is, they were connected men, and they were in Detroit on Tony Pro's orders.

The slender guy handed me the keys to the Mercury, gave me a scrap of paper with two sets of directions scribbled on one side. He explained that we were to drive out to a construction site a couple miles away and find the lot marked with the address 3237 Sibley Lane. We were to dig a hole, anywhere between the concrete forms of the house being built on the lot. It didn't have to be deep, he said. Just deep enough to hold the guy. A concrete crew would pour over the spot first thing in the morning, he said.

The second address was to a house back in Metro Detroit where we were supposed to leave the Mercury, once the contents of the trunk had been dealt with.

The guy got into the passenger seat of the Lincoln, and it drove away, kicking up a cloud of dust around us. I never saw the car or the guy again. I assumed both men went back to New Jersey, and I never thought much more about them.

We left my car on the side of the road and drove the Mercury, and its unwilling passenger, out to Sibley Lane, then left Mr. H in a hole as directed. Vince drove the Mercury to the address in Detroit, and me and Johnny picked him up in my car. Afterward, we went back to my place, had a few more beers, then called it a night.

I awoke the next day to learn the Tigers had lost by one run. The other big news of the day was that everyone was looking for Mr. H., and within another day or two, every friggin' whackjob in America had come to search Detroit for him, some armed with shovels, digging in every patch of dirt they encountered.

It didn't matter. They weren't gonna find him because by the time Mr. H's son was on TV asking for anyone who knew anything to come forward, the concrete above Mr. H's Sibley Lane resting place was already curing.

Johnny tossed his shovel aside and shouted, "I've got something."

He dug carefully with his gloved hands, pushing the dirt aside into mounds on the perimeter of the square hole. Shovels are destructive to things like old bones, and we needed to be sure we found all of Mr. H. Every single bone, any scrap of clothing that hadn't disintegrated over the last several decades. We had to find, and remove, anything that might cause a swimming pool installation crew to stop their work and call the cops.

Big Vince and I stood to the side, watching Johnny move sections of the earth below. Mixed into the soil were what might have been strands of cloth—resilient pieces of clothing that had survived the elements. He set them aside, then dug deeper, revealing what might have been a piece of an old shoe, perhaps a piece of one of Mr. H's Gucci loafers.

Whatever it was, it was worth taking out of the hole. Back then, we didn't think about things like DNA. With today's technology, some underpaid government scientist could probably figure out that me and my guys had put the friggin' body there. That's how they determined that Mr. H had been in the Mercury in the first place. A dog sniffed out his scent, but decades later, they tested a strand of hair collected from his old hairbrush and matched it to a hair found in the Mercury.

That's what we'd come for: to move Mr. H, and to remove anything that linked us to putting him there.

Johnny dug a little deeper, reached under the foundation a bit, and that's when he found it. An old Coke bottle.

It all came back to me. We'd been hitting the smokes and the Cokes hard all night. I'd finished drinking one as we dropped Mr. H in the hole, and I'd tossed it in with him before we covered him with dirt—and later concrete.

That friggin' bottle kept me awake for many nights after the hairbrush DNA thing. Hell, I thought about rounding the guys up on several occasions—thought about digging in the Zekman's basement to retrieve that goddamned bottle, along with my DNA that was on it. That stupid bottle, the one thing that could prove I was involved in the whole thing.

Johnny set the bottle aside and dug some more, and some more. "That's it, guys."

I leaned in, looked in the hole. "What d'ya mean that's it? Where's the body?"

"No idea." Johnny looked up at me, met my eyes with his. "It ain't here, that much I do know."

I didn't believe him, or maybe I'd lost trust in him. Either way, I stepped over the piles of dirt and climbed into the hole to take a look for myself. I dug new holes, I dug through the piles of dirt he'd made, I even dug under the concrete for several feet, expecting to find at least one small bone, or maybe more pieces of his shoes. But Johnny was right. Mr. H wasn't there.

We had the right spot. I knew we did because of the coke bottle. I looked up at the guys, shook my head in disbelief. "Where the hell is he?"

Vince shook his head. "That section of concrete looked weird when I cut into it."

Sitting back, resting against a mound of dirt I said, "Looked weird in what way?"

"It was discolored. It cut differently too. Like it wasn't the same material as the rest."

"You tellin' me that someone's already been here, and that they've already done what we're here to do?"

Vince shrugged. "I'm just sayin' it looked weird when I cut it, that's all."

Johnny peered out the high basement window that faced the street. "Hey, Gino. A lot more people are gathering out there. I think they're getting suspicious. You and your *finesse* had better get out there and talk them down."

I stood up, pushed a mound of dirt back into the hole. "What's the point? We're done here."

Johnny turned to look at me. "You serious?"

"The body's gone. What's the point of sticking around? Unless you're looking to get arrested."

We packed up our tools and shoved some of the dirt back in the hole. I had a story worked out that I'd tell Mrs. Zekman—a bunch of bullshit about how Consumers Energy would send out another crew who'd patch up the concrete.

Before heading up the stairs, I grabbed the old Coke bottle. It'd probably fetch a few bucks on eBay, but it had tons of sentimental value to me. It was, after all, my only tangible link to that July evening.

Sure, it bothered me that Mr. H wasn't there. But wondering who moved him bothered me more. Maybe the boss didn't trust us as much as I thought. Or maybe the boss had his own DNA concerns once the hairbrush thing hit the news; maybe he had another crew come out and relocate Mr. H to avoid having to do it last minute. The important part was that Mr. H wasn't there, and with the body gone, me and my guys couldn't be linked to any of it.

Mrs. Zekman was standing at the edge of her driveway. Seeing us exit with all our gear had given her hope that she could return to her home.

I tossed a bag into the back of the truck, then walked over to her. "You're all set, ma'am."

"Oh, good. I can go back in now? Is it safe?"

"One hundred percent. We found the leak, and we patched it. You shouldn't have any more troubles."

"Oh, thank you. That's good to hear."

"We did have to break up some of your concrete in the basement, but at least it was in an area that didn't have any carpet. Still, I'm sorry about the mess. Someone will give you a call later, and they'll send out a crew that'll get that patched up for you. Make it good as new."

"Oh, there's no need. We're having a pool installed next week. They're going to dig up the concrete anyhow."

I smiled. "A pool? Wow. That sounds nice. Well, in that case, I'll let the folks at HQ know that there's no need to send a repair crew to your home, but I'll let 'em know that the sidewalk still needs patching."

"Thank you. And thank you so much for the work you do. It sounds like you saved our house from blowing up. You gentlemen are heroes."

I glanced at Vince, then at Johnny. "Not at all, ma'am. We're just good soldiers who do what we're told." I tipped my hardhat to her. "You have a great rest of your day, and hey, enjoy that pool."

We drove away with half of Sibley Lane waving at us like we were war veterans in a town parade. We ditched the truck and the backhoe over in Pontiac, a few miles from where we'd stolen them to begin with. That night we drank some beers at my place and burned the work shirts and the pieces of the shoe in the fireplace.

I held onto the bottle though. Kept it on my mantel for many years as a little reminder of that night, and of my guys.

Vince passed away a few years back. Big fella's heart eventually gave out. Johnny, he's gone too. His liver finally had all the booze it could take.

When they passed, I tucked the bottle away in an old cedar chest, along with a handful of other keepsakes that meant a little something to me. I shoved this little note down the bottle's neck, which is probably how you, or the folks at the estate auction, got hold of it. No matter who found it, if you're reading this, it means the damned lung cancer finally beat me. It also means you know as much as I ever knew about what happened to ol' Mr. H, wherever the hell he is.

LUXURY GOODS

She nearly whispered the order to the bartender. Virgin mojito, extra mint. Bars are unpopular places to not drink alcohol.

It was a nice place. Modern and trendy with funky carpets, pops of color everywhere, and lots of mid-century modern touches. Smooth jazz played softly from speakers tucked into the high ceilings as the bartender placed a napkin on the bar in front of her. Moments later, he set her drink on the napkin.

Settling into one of the padded stools, she sipped the drink, allowing the minty taste to transport her to an exotic location, someplace more interesting than a hotel bar near the airport.

Reaching for her cell phone, she offered a quick smile to the man at the end of the bar. He'd been staring at her since she walked in. Now he'd moved on from staring to checking her up and down. Nothing about her outfit was provocative, just a dark blue flare dress with a split collar. For a plain button-up dress, it always seemed to gain lots of attention from guys, probably because it had a schoolgirl look to it, which seemed to ignite a particular fantasy in their minds.

From her periphery, she noticed his eyes had shifted to her knee-high suede boots. For a moment, at least. His eyes soon began scanning up her legs, then to her ass, then to her breasts.

She could move, sure. Maybe grab a table somewhere out of his gaze, but he seemed harmless. Probably just a lonely, horny business traveler.

She looked at him. He seemed embarrassed that she'd caught him staring at her chest. She offered another slight smile before returning her attention to her phone.

He was attractive, even if his hairline was beginning to betray him. He wasn't handsome or stunning, necessarily, but he seemed to be in good shape. He was, however, probably close to double her age. She guessed late forties, maybe early fifties. So maybe not double her age, but even if he was only forty-five, that still meant eighteen years separated them, which was probably exciting for him.

Laughing to herself about men and their weird thoughts, she returned to her phone and began mindlessly scrolling through Instagram, dream-shopping for a new wardrobe for this summer, which was still a good three months away.

It seemed he'd taken her last smile as some kind of invitation and was now standing to her right, a couple stool-lengths away. She pretended not to notice.

Eventually he said, "You just passing through too, I take it?"

It was an awkward pick-up line, but probably not for a guy his age. She turned her head to him and said, "I'm sorry?"

"Oh, I was just wondering if you're staying here on business, or if you're from the area."

She offered him another smile, a reward for putting a pathetic spin on the classic "are you from around here?"

He seemed like a nice guy, so she went along with his attempt at conversation and said, "I'm waiting for a flight."

He smiled an awkward smile, his teeth straight and bright, likely the result of regular whitening treatments. She smiled back and threw him an easy one, saying, "How about you? Business travel?"

"Yeah. Third time this month I've been here."

The TravisMathew shirt he wore said that he probably liked golf, and the well-fitted dress slacks it was paired with along with the Ted Baker belt indicated a woman probably selected his outfits for him.

He leaned against the bar and said, "So, you traveling for business as well?"

"No. I'm trying to get back to New England after visiting my grandmother in Florida. I was supposed to grab a connecting flight here, so I ran across the airport—in heeled boots nonetheless—to have someone at the gate tell me that my flight had been canceled. So, I'm stranded here until tomorrow."

"Oh, wow. That sucks. I've had that happen." He laughed a fake laugh. "I mean, not the running in heels part."

She pretended to laugh.

He motioned to an empty stool. "You mind?"

She shook her head, and he pulled out the stool. Once settled, he extended his hand and said, "I'm Steven."

She shook his hand. "Jess."

"Nice to meet you, Jess. Sorry your trip isn't going well."

"I've only told you the first part." She chuckled darkly. "Most of my luggage is on its way to a city I'm not in. Then, I'd thought I'd gotten a reservation at a hotel, so I took an Uber there only to learn they somehow didn't have me in their system, and the place was booked solid. So, then I Ubered over here, and luckily, I got a room, but when I got to the room, I realized I didn't have my debit card. The last place I remember having it was the first Uber, but I haven't been able to get hold of that driver, so I ended up just canceling the card."

He exhaled a long breath slowly. "Okay. That takes the cake. For as much as I've traveled, I don't think I've ever had a day that bad. You were able to get a room though? Even without your card?"

"Yeah. It was just my debit card, and thankfully my credit card was still in my bag." She motioned to the brown leather Coach bag on the stool next to her. "But needless to say, it's been a long day."

"I'm very sorry."

He asked where she was from, and she told him Portland, Maine. He'd never been, but he'd like to visit because he'd heard it was beautiful. She told him it was. Steven was from Northern California, a town named Lodi in between Sacramento and Stockton. He liked it, he said.

Finishing a sip of his drink, he said, "The weather's about perfect. Wish it was closer to a good beach though."

She nodded and sipped her drink. The gold Michael Kors chronograph on his wrist looked nice, though it probably wasn't too expensive. His entire outfit could be purchased at any Nordstrom store, but this guy probably got it all at an outlet mall. Even more likely, his wife got it there. Though he wasn't wearing a wedding ring, the white line on his ring finger indicated he usually wore one while golfing in the California sunshine.

Her drink empty, she pushed it away and said, "I'd love to live near a sunny beach."

Steven nodded, then took a look around the bar. "Let's grab a table. What d'you say?"

Before she could answer, Steven flagged down the bartender, told him to put her drinks on his tab, and ordered a second round.

Steven grabbed his drink—a single malt scotch on the rocks—and stood up to search for a table, ultimately selecting a booth along the wall.

He motioned for her to sit. She set her bag in the corner, tucked her dress, and scooted across the leather-like surface.

He scooted in next to her, instead of taking one of the open chairs across the table. Steven's game was improving, and that brought a slight smile to her face.

They talked about hometowns—how she's originally from Virginia and how he's always lived in California. They talked about travel, how flying places used to be kind of fun. She told him she managed a small boutique, and how it doesn't pay well, but she gets a great discount on awesome clothes. He talked about his consulting work with companies all over the country.

By the third round of drinks, Steven had gotten pretty handsy, comfortably resting his palm on her thigh as they talked about how both of them had flights tomorrow. He hadn't asked yet, but he was definitely interested in taking things upstairs to his room. In his mind, it was the only possible outcome of this chance encounter—they're both in town tonight, neither have anywhere to go until tomorrow—so sex was the obvious thing to fill the time in between.

She expected him to make a move, or at least hint at going to his room, but then he began telling a story about how the last time he was in town it was during a major convention, and he had to book a hotel almost an hour away to even get a room.

Jess wasn't really listening though. She was distracted by the woman at the table across from them. She'd just arrived, and she was talking loudly on her phone, clearly upset about something.

Steven noticed too, and soon his eyes also shifted to the woman. After a moment, he said, "What's going on?"

Jess shook her head. "I don't know. She seems really upset."

The woman was gorgeous and young, around twenty-five. Her skin olive and perfect, her long brown hair draped across her delicate shoulders as if it had been painted there.

Her outfit was as stunning as she was—expensive designer jeans, a simple V-neck tee with a black blazer over it. The tee was probably two hundred dollars; the jeans at least five hundred. But the real eye-catcher was the Francesco Russo ankle strap pumps on her feet. They had to set her back at least eight hundred.

Jess and Steven watched her as she collapsed into a chair, tossing a leather Louboutin tote bag on the table, its signature red bottom adding one more pop of color to the trendy bar.

With one elbow on the table, the woman rested her head on her hand as she said, "I don't know what I'm going to do. I can't change my flight at this point."

She spoke with a British accent, her voice soft and soothing to the ears, even though she was in distress.

Finishing her phone call, she rested her head on both hands looking as though she might cry.

Jess spoke loudly across the table, "Excuse me. Are you all right?"

The woman didn't respond for a moment, but then she turned to look their way, wearing a look of surprise that a stranger was interested in her problems. She nodded and said, "Oh, yes. Thank you." Her accent made her more intriguing, and her stunning green eyes almost seemed backlit.

Steven stared at her for a moment, then returned his attention to Jess and restarted his story.

The woman stood and came to their table. Interrupting Steven, she said, "Actually, things aren't going so well. I don't suppose either of you would be keen on buying a bag or wallet, would you? It's excellent stuff, really. Designer stuff. Saint Laurent. I've got a shoulder bag and a beautiful, pebbled calfskin wallet I need to sell."

Jess glanced at Steven, then returned her attention to the woman standing at their table, "Why are you selling them?"

"I'm afraid it's quite a story, really. You see, it's my job. I'm a sales rep for a luxury retailer in London. I'm in the States to meet some buyers—in fact, I was supposed to meet one just now, but they've gone and canceled on me. So now, I'm stuck with these bags—which I've paid nearly seventeen hundred US for."

She grabbed the tote bag off the table and pulled the shoulder bag and wallet out for them to see. "My flight leaves tonight, and I can't get on the plane with these. If I take them back to London with me, I'll have to pay import duties. I can't say how much that'll be exactly, but it would be phenomenal, I'm sure."

Steven shook his head. "I'm sorry, but we're not interested."

The woman's shoulders slumped. "Are you certain? If you'd buy these from me for seventeen hundred dollars, you could list them on eBay for twice that much, easily. They'd sell in a matter of hours. I'd do it myself if I didn't have a flight to catch."

Steven went quiet. He seemed to be thinking about it. "Twice that amount?"

The woman nodded and said, "Without a doubt."

Steven's hand slid from Jess's leg and into his pocket. Under the table, out of the woman's view, he checked the amount of cash he had, then said, "They're really worth that much?"

The woman nodded. "Most definitely." Sliding into the booth next to Steven, she laid the merchandise on the table in front of him. Holding up the shoulder bag, she said, "This one here. It retails for twenty three hundred dollars."

Steven took the bag and examined it closely.

The woman held up the wallet and said, "This here, this one retails for about eleven hundred."

Steven set the shoulder bag on the table and took the wallet from her. He opened the flap, then traced the edges with the pad of his thumb.

The woman leaned over, making eye contact with Jess. She said, "I'm sorry. I'm afraid I've been quite rude. My name is Chloe."

Jess introduced herself, Steven too. He stared at the goods, his mind likely busy thinking about the potential profit. Then he said, "I can give you eight hundred."

Chloe gasped slightly then said, "For both?"

Steven nodded.

"I'm afraid I can't do that." Chloe took the bags back, then stood up. "That's a bigger loss than the duties I'd have to pay. I'm sorry. And I'm sorry to have bothered you. Thank you both for your time."

Chloe fumbled to get the bag and wallet back into the tote bag, and Steven said, "Hold on." He patted the booth next to him where she'd been seated. "Please, stay. We'll get some drinks, and we'll see if we can work out a price that works for both of us."

Chloe smiled, then sat beside Steven. Within seconds his other hand found its way to Chloe's thigh. His full attention shifted to her as well, as though Jess were no longer sitting on the other side of him.

Steven caught the attention of a waitress and ordered himself a beer as Chloe checked out the wine selections. Looking up from the menu, she said, "I'll have a glass of the Merry Edwards pinot noir, please."

Jess nodded in agreement. "That sounds perfect. I'll have the same."

Steven's hand was back on Jess's leg, his other arm thrown over the back of the booth ensuring it was out of the way so Chloe could get as close as she'd like.

They'd stopped talking about Yves Saint Laurent accessories. He was now peppering Chloe with questions about London. He'd never been, but maybe she could show him around someday. She laughed, scooted closer, and agreed.

Steven squeezed Jess's thigh, turned his head toward her and said, "Maybe she could show both of us around, right?"

Jess smiled and said, "Now that could be fun."

Steven smiled a big grin.

He seemed in no hurry to work out a deal on the bag and wallet. He wanted to know more about Chloe. Where in England she'd grown up. What she did in her spare time. And he acted shocked when she said she didn't have a boyfriend.

"I travel a lot for work," she said. "Haven't got the time, I guess."

Steven nodded an understanding nod, then said, "I know what that's like. I feel like I'm in a different city every day."

Their drinks arrived and Steven settled deeper into the padded booth, now wrapping his other arm around Jess's shoulders. The three chatted, and Steven laughed loudly at things that weren't funny, an obvious ploy to gain the attention of the other patrons who'd begun filing into the bar at the end of the workday. This was clearly the highest point in his life—drinking in a fancy bar with two young, beautiful women at his side. He wanted everyone to notice.

Steven ordered another round of drinks. He wiped beer from his mouth and said, "All right then, let's see what we can work out for these bags."

Chloe had brought it up at least twice during the second round of drinks, but Steven was clearly relishing the time with both of them and hadn't wanted to discuss matters of money. But as they waited for another round of drinks to come, it seemed he welcomed the conversation to fill the time between beers.

Steven picked the YSL wallet up and examined it. "You really need seventeen hundred bucks for these, huh?"

Chloe nodded and said, "That's my cost. I'd really like to break even, you know? Like I said, you'd be able to get a lot more for them."

"How do I know these aren't fakes? I mean, I'm not accusing you of anything, but I have to admit, I don't know shit about things like this." He laughed, loudly. "These could have come from Walmart, and I'd never know the difference." Another loud laugh.

Chloe took the wallet from him, folded back the flap, and said, "Look inside. Each one's got a serial number, and the style number. You can look that up on their website."

He examined it closely and said, "Made in Italy, huh?" He thought for a moment and then said, "But still, that stuff's easy to fake, right?"

Jess decided to speak up. "Look at the stitching."

He looked at her, his eyebrows raised with surprise. "Oh yeah? What about it?"

She took the wallet from him and ran her finger across the side. "The stitching on this is very straight. Counterfeiters don't put that kind of effort in."

Steven took the wallet and examined the stitching closely. "Yeah, that is straight."

Jess nodded, then picked up the shoulder bag. The leather is high quality too. Look at the sheen. It's real, and it's a great quality leather. Again, counterfeiters don't use quality materials like this."

Steven nodded as he took the bag from her. He looked at it briefly before saying to Chloe, "Jess knows this stuff pretty good. She sells this kind of stuff."

Chloe leaned into the table to speak to Jess, "Oh yeah? Are you in the industry?"

Jess nodded and said, "I run a boutique. We sell lots of luxury items."

"Fabulous." Chloe smiled. "Then this is perfect. If you have any trouble selling these online, perhaps you could sell them in your store? You could surely get the full retail price there."

Steven seemed happy about the prospect. He turned to Jess and said, "That could work. What d'you think? It'd give me a reason to come visit you in Maine."

She smiled and said, "I could sell them fast."

"You think you can get the full price?"

Jess took the handbag and looked inside, then checked out the wallet. "How much did you say they're worth?"

Chloe leaned in again and said, "Twenty three hundred for the bag, and eleven hundred for the chained wallet."

Steven had his phone out, already looking them up online. He clicked a few links and then said, "She's not kidding. I had no idea these things were so expensive."

Jess set them both on the table and slid them toward Chloe. She turned to Steven and said, "I know two or three customers who'd want these. I might even be able to call them in the morning and arrange a sale through the phone."

Steven reached into his pocket and pulled out the wad of cash again. Counting out the bills, he placed them on the table in front of him. "I've got eight hundred on me. Well, that and seven in singles." He turned to Jess. "Sorry to ask, sweetie, but do you have anything on you?"

Jess reached into her bag and retrieved her wallet. She dug out the cash inside and set it on the table. "Twenty bucks. That's all I've got."

Chloe sighed, then slid the YSL bags back into her tote. "Well, thank you both very much. I'm afraid I just can't sell them for that amount. I quite appreciate your time though."

Jess placed her hand on Steven's leg and said, "What about an ATM? There's probably one in the hotel lobby."

Steven thought about it for a moment, then said, "Okay. Let's go see, shall we, sweetie?"

Jess nodded.

Chloe stood so they could get out of the booth.

Jess slid out and stood beside Steven. He leaned into Chloe and said, "We'll hit the ATM. Why don't you flag that waitress down and get us some more drinks."

They walked in silence until they were across the lobby. At the ATM, Steven looked across the room toward the bar. Secure in the idea that Chloe couldn't hear him, he said, "You're sure those are the real deal?"

Jess nodded and said, "Definitely. The leather is great quality, and the stitching too. The logos are nicely centered and clean. That's never the case with fakes.

Honestly, if they're fakes, then they're the best I've ever seen. And if that's the case, my customers won't know either."

He thought it over briefly and then said, "So, you're sure we can get the full thirty four hundred for them?"

"At least close to it. Three grand, for sure."

"How quickly could you sell 'em?"

"By the end of the week, for sure. Probably a lot quicker though. A few of my regular customers love stuff like that. I can make a few phone calls tomorrow, and I may even have them sold before the end of the day."

"People are that crazy for this stuff, huh?"

Jess shrugged. "What can I say? Girls like pretty things."

His hands on his hips, Steven thought about it, then turned to the ATM and slid his card into the slot. After a few beeps, the machine spit out several bills. Steven took a quick count then said, "I've got an idea."

He'd piqued her interest for sure. "What kind of an idea?"

"If we pay her seventeen hundred, then sell them for three grand, that's a profit of thirteen hundred, which is not a bad profit at all."

"Seems good to me."

He nodded and said, "But she seems desperate to sell these things. That puts us in a good position to get a better deal." He held up the wad of cash. "I only pulled out five hundred. That's a total of thirteen hundred bucks. I'm thinking we tell her that my bank limited me to five hundred. If she thinks all we've got is thirteen hundred, she'll take it. Thirteen hundred seems like a fair price to me."

Jess nodded in agreement. "I guess so, but what if she walks away altogether?"

"I don't think she will." He began to walk back to the bar.

She grabbed his arm and said, "Wait."

Steven turned to face her, his face covered in confusion.

Jess stroked his arm and said, "I have a backup plan. Pull out another four hundred. I'll hang onto it, and if she won't take our deal, then I'll get up and pretend to go to the ATM. She doesn't know I don't have a debit card."

Steven thought it over, staring off toward the entrance. Finally, he said, "Okay, yeah. That's smart."

Chloe was sipping a glass of brandy when they returned to the table. A matching glass awaited Jess, and another scotch on the rocks sat for Steven. In the center of the table, three shot glasses filled with something awaited them.

Jess sat down in one of the chairs and took a sip of brandy. It was quality, for sure. Chloe definitely knew her booze.

Chloe was happy. Smiling. Certain she was about to get her money and be on her way. She laughed, and giggled, then pulled Steven down into the booth to sit beside her.

Chloe grabbed one of the shot glasses and said, "Let's celebrate, yes?"

Steven looked sad. He rubbed Chloe's thigh and said, "Sorry. Um, the ATM limited me to five hundred." He pulled the cash from his pocket and set it on the table. "The best I can do is thirteen hundred."

Chloe sipped her drink as she thought it over. "There's no way you can get the other four hundred? Can you call your bank or something?"

"Sorry. I tried. They said they can't change the limit for twenty four hours. Some kind of security safeguard, I guess."

A wave of respect for Steven washed over Jess. He was much quicker on his feet than she'd given him credit for.

Chloe looked at Jess. "How about you? Is there any way you can make up the difference?"

Before she could answer, Steven said, "I'm sorry. I'd really love to help you out, but I'm afraid thirteen is the best we can do."

Jess sipped her brandy as Chloe contemplated the cash that was literally on the table.

Chloe finished the last drink of her brandy, patted Steven's hand, then stood up. "Well, thank you for trying." Grabbing her gorgeous Louboutin tote, she flung the strap over her shoulder and said, "I really need the full amount, and I'd better get going. I can't miss my flight."

Jess finished the brandy and said, "Chloe, wait." She grabbed her bag off the table. "Let me go to the ATM. I'll see if I can make up the difference."

"Yeah?" A wide smile filled Chloe's youthful face. "I quite appreciate that."

Jess walked out of the bar and into the lobby. Once she was around the corner, she leaned against the wall and retrieved her phone from her bag. No one had called or messaged. She scrolled through Facebook a little. Nothing too new. Her friend Monica got a new puppy. Emily's little girl was walking now, apparently.

Jess dropped her phone back into her bag and retrieved the cash Steven had given her.

Walking back into the bar, she found Steven nestled up close to Chloe. Again, he laughed loudly.

Jess held the cash up so Chloe could see it. "Four hundred. That gives you the full seventeen hundred."

Chloe stood up and hugged Jess. "Thank you so much, love. Oh, I can't tell you how great you both are." Chloe grabbed the stack of cash Steven had set on the table, then took the cash from Jess's hand.

Chloe finished counting the money, then produced a small Manila envelope from her tote bag. She slid the cash inside the envelope, then slid the envelope into the inside pocket of her blazer. "This is cause for celebration, yes?" She motioned toward the shots on the table. "I took the liberty of ordering us tequila. I hope that's okay."

Steven pulled her onto the bench seat, almost into his lap. "That's perfect." He picked up one of the shots, held it into the air and said, "To Chloe. May she have a safe trip back to London."

They all raised their shots, then tossed them back. It had a smooth taste, especially for tequila.

Chloe stood again, picked up the tote bag and said, "I guess these are yours now." She reached in and began to pull the YSL bags out, then paused. "Unless..." She thought for a moment. "Yes, I can't believe I didn't think about this earlier. I've got two other bags up in my room. Maybe you'd like those better? One's a Louis Vuitton. I could swap that one for the wallet, maybe. Since you're helping me out so much. It's worth quite a bit more than the wallet. You'd make a bigger profit."

Steven shook his head. Before he could speak, Jess said, "I wouldn't mind seeing the Louis Vuitton, for sure."

She felt Steven shooting her a look, but she ignored him, keeping her focus on Chloe, who said, "Yeah? Okay, let me go grab it real quick." She began to walk away, but Jess stopped her.

"Wait. You're not taking our cash *and* the bags, are you?"

"Oh, my." Chloe reached into her jacket pocket and pulled out the envelope. "I wasn't thinking. My apologies." She set the envelope on the table. "I'll leave that right there. I'll only be a few moments."

Steven stood. "I'll go with you."

Chloe stepped close to him, her face inches from his. "I'm sorry, love. I don't let men into my room. You can understand, can't you?"

Steven nearly smiled, despite being turned down, seemingly intoxicated by her flirting.

Jess interrupted and said, "I'll go with you then."

Chloe turned toward her. "Oh, okay. Sure thing, love."

Jess grabbed her bag and said, "I'm sorry. I don't mean to imply that you're some kind of con artist or something, but we did just meet you."

"No offense taken." Chloe smiled. "Shall we, then?" Jess glanced at Steven. He nodded slightly, then patted the envelope on the table. She nodded at Chloe and said, "Okay. Let's see this Louis Vuitton."

Steven sipped his scotch as the two walked out of the bar. In the lobby, Chloe laughed and said, "Don't you think the con artist line was a bit much?"

Jess chuckled. "I thought it was funny."

"It was a bit much." Chloe's British accent was gone.

"You're dropping the accent already?"

"You like that, do you?"

"It has a certain appeal."

Chloe smiled, and with the accent she said, "Sure thing, governor."

As they walked out through the big sliding doors to the parking lot, Jess gave a look over her shoulder. It seemed Steven was a good boy and had stayed like he'd been told. The waitress should be bringing his bill around soon, which would be a shock.

As they approached the car, Jess said, "How much was that brandy?"

Chloe laughed. "Technically, it was cognac. Remy Martin X.O. Thirty six bucks a glass."

"I see why. It was damn good." She tossed her bag in the back seat. "And the tequila?"

"Don Julio Real. I think that one was sixty five per shot. Hell, the pinot was twenty five a glass, and we had, what? Six of those between us. Plus, I'm guessing he picked up your initial drinks. Virgin mojito, I assume?"

"Three of them."

Chloe rolled her eyes. "Virgin though?"

"Got to keep my wits about me. What if I were to get drunk and run off with the guy?"

Chloe laughed, then said "Oh, shit." She set the tote bag on the roof. "I almost forgot." She produced a bottle of wine from the bag.

"Where'd that come from?"

"I ordered it when you two went to the ATM machine. I told them we were going to drink it in the room, so we didn't need glasses. Waitress thought nothing of it when I put it in my bag."

Jess smiled. "Nice touch."

Chloe inspected it. "Chambolle-Musigny. It's a twenty twelve."

"What'd that set him back?"

"Two-forty, I think?"

Chloe reached into her pocket, grabbed the envelope, then tossed it to Jess. "You want to look after that for us?"

After draping her blazer over the back of the driver's seat, Chloe sat down and started the car. Jess sat in the passenger seat and took a look at the cash. By now, Steven was surely growing impatient with how long they'd been gone. In their absence, he'd finish his drink. He'd eventually look at the envelope on the table, poke at it with his thick fingers, spin it on the table in front of him.

He'd look toward the bar entrance, wondering what's taking them so damn long (women, right?). He'd poke at the envelope some more until curiosity and suspicion took over and forced him to open it.

Plunging his fingers inside, he'd pull out the contents. His jaw would drop as he realized there's no cash inside, just a stack of neatly trimmed clippings from an old Vogue magazine. He'd slam the envelope on the table as he wondered how, and when, Chloe made the switch.

Jess smiled to herself as she pictured it. Leaning over, she kissed Chloe on the cheek. "Thanks for a fun night."

"Anytime." Chloe smiled as she exited the parking lot and drove away from the hotel.

Jess watched the city pass by them out the car window. About now, Steven was probably trying to figure out what happened. Replaying the entire evening, realizing Jess was in on it all along, and wondering how he let it happen.

The worst part wasn't even over for him. He'd settle the bar tab, somehow. He'd eventually get over the loss of seventeen hundred dollars in cash. But what he probably hadn't thought about yet was his wife. How long would it be until she learned about the credit card charges, or the ATM withdrawals? A couple grand spent on a few hours in a hotel bar with two beautiful girls he never had a shot with. To a guy like Steven, that probably seemed like a fair price.

FLUSH

The sound of my toilet gurgling, and the sight of water overflowing onto my bathroom floor, forced me out of bed earlier than planned. I own exactly two bath towels, and both now lay on my floor, soaked with toilet water—part of my futile attempt to keep the water from reaching the carpet in the hallway.

This has happened four times in the few months I've lived in this dump. I reported the problem to my landlord the last three times, and each time, he said he'd have someone come out and look at the plumbing.

It hasn't happened yet.

My landlord lives on a golf course in Arizona. I live in a one-bed unit in a shitty building he owns in Chicago's North Lawndale neighborhood. There's no golf course around here, but I do have a stunning view of two abandoned buildings and an old gas station. This being the case, to say that my landlord doesn't care about my toilet problems would be a massive understatement.

My previous landlord was the Illinois Department of Corrections where I lived for nineteen months, and I have to say, some days, this shithole apartment makes me miss prison.

My current landlord ain't going to fix this problem, and there ain't much I can do about that. He's a cheap son of a bitch, but I tolerate him because he's also what you might call "morally flexible." You see, given who my last landlord was, it's not easy finding a place to live, and while his rental applications do ask about felony convictions, if you slip him a little extra during the application process, he doesn't run a background check on you. So it's like that old saying about beggars being choosy.

Anyway, I drive the plunger into the toilet bowl, my only hope of unclogging this thing, but that sends even more water over the edge and onto the floor. There's no turning back now, so I thrust it in deeper and the toilet bubbles. I pump the plunger and hear one more loud gurgling noise as the rest of the water flows effortlessly down the drain, leaving me to deal with the soggy floor.

My phone rings as I wade into the mess. It's my burner, so I figure it's Nate.

"Yeah?"

"Jimmy?"

"The one and only."

"You busy?"

Glancing at my soaked floor I say, "Busy living the dream."

"Cool, cool. Did you think about it?"

"Yeah, I thought about it."

"And?"

"And I need to think about it some more."

"Understood, dog, but this can't wait forever. He'll need an answer soon. If you're not in, he's gonna have to find somebody else."

"I'll let you know soon."

"Cool, cool. Well, I'll let you get back to it."

I toss the phone onto the countertop as I assess the damage to the carpet. It's soaked down to the pad. I've got a couple fans I can put down to dry the surface, but beyond that, I've got no good way to get the water out of the pad. I'm also supposed to be at work in about an hour, so I don't have time to deal with this shit. And I can't mess around with my job because, for a felon, finding a place to live is hard, but finding a job is even harder. That's why I'm stuck working the graveyard. It sucks, but in less than two months, I'll finally be off supervised release, and then my life belongs to me again. Until then, if I'm late, even once, they could drop me, which could be considered a violation of my release.

I got no idea what to tell Nate. He's asking me to risk a lot on a stranger—some guy he did time with in county. The guy has a job that requires my particular expertise, and it's supposedly lucrative as hell. Nearly six figures, he claims.

But there's a catch: the cash currently belongs to some cops from the 'burbs. Apparently they've been running a side hustle ripping off drug traffickers. Seems they've been successful at it too, because now they're sitting on so much cash that they can't spend it all without drawing attention to their naughty behavior. So instead, they've stashed tens of thousands of dollars inside some auto detailing shop out by O'Hare while they make other arrangements.

It's tempting, of course. Even after a split with this guy and a finder's fee for Nate, I could walk away with fifty grand. Plus we get to rip off some dipshit cops.

On the other hand, there's a lot that could go wrong. If we get caught, my ass goes back to prison on a violation, plus whatever else they charge me with. And we're talking about cops here, so if they catch on to us, they could bust us themselves. But they're not *just* cops, they're *dirty* cops, so they could just as easily shoot us in the back of the head and dump our bodies in the woods before getting a beer together.

I also don't know much about this guy other than his name is Ty and that he and Nate shared a cell for a couple months. I'd be risking a whole lot on someone I know very little about.

Nate agreed to meet during my break. None of this should be discussed over the phone, and I have a lot of questions.

I clock out just after midnight and head to the edge of the parking lot. As I walk to Nate's car, I see him sitting on the edge of the bumper with someone beside him.

Nate stands and greets me with a fist bump. "Good to see you, dog." He nods toward the skinny guy next to him. "This is my boy, Ty."

We exchange a quick handshake and say "hey" to each other, then Nate says, "Ty should have all the answers you need."

I start with the most basic question. "How much cash are we talking?"

"At least eighty or ninety grand." Ty steps closer to me. "It's just sitting there waitin' for us, bro. And my man Nate here says you a genius safecracker or whatever."

He flatters. In reality, I'm the criminal son of a locksmith named James O'Shea Sr., a man who disowned me years ago. But if the point he's trying to make is that I'm good at getting into safes, I won't argue. "The cash, it's in a safe?"

Ty nods. "A big one. Like a gun safe or whatever."

One big question has been on my mind for a while, so I say, "Nate told me that we'd be hitting cops. I'm wondering how you know these guys?"

"I've never met 'em, bro. There's no way I'd hit 'em if I knew 'em, you know what I'm sayin'?"

"That takes us to my next question: how do you know about their side hustle?"

"Let's just say a buddy of mine brought it to my attention."

I turn to Nate and say, "You forget to mention there's a fourth guy involved?"

"Hey, man, this is the first I'm hearing about it, I swear."

Returning my attention to Ty I say, "This fourth dude got a name?"

"They call him Wookiee."

"Wookiee?"

"Yeah, 'cause he real harry an' shit."

Losing patience I say, "How do you know this furry motherfucker?"

"We did some time together. I've run into him here and there over the years, you know what I'm sayin'?"

"And how is it that this guy you've done time with happens to know that a group of cops are ripping off drug dealers?"

"It's like this, homie: Wookiee's good at cards, so these pigs be inviting him to play with 'em. See, they hang out in the back of this auto body shop. It's owned by one of them's brothers, and they all hang out there at night. They hold poker games there, and my man Wookiee, he been to a bunch of 'em. He's peeked in the safe a buncha times, and bro, the cash just keeps stacking up." His head droops. "But Wookiee... I ain't seen him in a while. I've been hearing things—hearing that these pigs accused him of cheating 'em, and I don't know what happened to him."

"So you're looking for revenge?"

"I mean, sorta, bro, but I also see opportunity, you know what I'm sayin'? Like, this shit just fell into my lap and I gotta take it."

I turn to Nate and say, "I don't do the revenge thing. I'm out."

"You sure, dog?"

"Yeah, I'm sure." I turn away to head back inside, but Ty stops me. "C'mon, homie. I can't do this without you. I'll up your cut to seventy five percent."

I stop walking and face him. "How much are we talking again? You said eighty to ninety grand total, right?"

He nods. "Easily, bro."

"So you're cool settling for something in the neighborhood of twenty grand?"

"For sure, bro. Like, I get it, you'd be doing most of the work. I'm cool with my cut being smaller."

"This cash. It's drug cash?"

"Yeah, bro. A shit-ton of it."

"How do you know it's drug money and not just poker funds?"

"I know people, bro. Everyone on the street know what these pigs be doin'. Nobody can do nothin' about it though, you know what I'm sayin'? They cops."

"Nate tells me we need to hit these guys in the next few days. Why can't we just wait a few weeks?"

"Wookiee overheard them talking, bro. They been working out some details to get the cash out of the country. A bank in the Caribbean, I think. Supposedly got flights booked next week. Once they get on those planes, the opportunity's gone."

"How do we know the cash will be there? What's to say they haven't already moved it?"

"I been sittin' on 'em, you know what I'm sayin'? Been watching 'em for a couple weeks now. They always be bringing big bags into that place. Cash. Lots of cash that's going into that safe. They stuck with all of it right now 'cause if they go spending it, they attract too much attention."

"You're sure about all of this intel?"

"Positive, bro."

I know I should walk away from this one, but damn it, I'm intrigued. "Let's talk access. Are there people around overnight?"

"No, man. The cops use the back room a few nights a week, but they usually out by like two, three a.m. Other than that, the place is open regular business hours."

"What's around it? Houses? Businesses? Truck stops, gas stations? Anything with potential witnesses?"

"Naw, bro. Nothing like that. It's just a bunch of warehouses an' whatever. Very industrial."

"Can you get me some details on the safe? Manufacturer's name, maybe the model? Maybe a couple photos?"

"I can work that out, yeah. That all you need, bro?"

"It's a start."

"Then what? How long you need to figure out the combo and all that?"

I chuckle. This dude must watch a lot of bad movies. "I don't plan on figuring out the combo. It's much quicker to drill it."

"That's it, bro? Damn, man. I can do that myself."

"Yeah? Okay. What type of bits will you use? Where are you going to drill?"

"I'll drill into, like, the lock, man."

"The lock's inside, behind several inches of steel, and probably protected by a hardened steel plate."

"No, not the lock. I mean, like, the keyhole."

"There likely won't be a keyhole on the type of safe you've described, but even if there is, drilling through it won't get you inside. Beyond that, the safe likely has a relocker, and if you drill too deep in the wrong spot, you'll trigger it, then the thing will be bolted shut nice and solid. How you going to deal with that?"

Ty's eyes narrow. He's confused, which I expected. Everyone thinks this stuff is easy, but it's not. It's why guys like Ty need guys like me.

Nate steps in and says, "Dog, I told you, my boy Jimmy knows his shit. I've watched him do this, yo. He knows all the tricks, and he's got all the tools."

Ty nods. "Yeah, yeah. I hear ya, bro." He turns to me. "Sorry, homie. I didn't mean no disrespect."

I nod and say, "So back to getting into the safe. I may need an hour, maybe longer, depending on the quality of the steel. And it won't be quiet. That gonna be a problem?"

"Not at all, bro. Like I said, it's super chill around there."

"You can get me some details on the safe then? Without at least some basic info, I'm not doing this."

"Yeah, yeah. I got you, homie."

"How?"

"What d'ya mean?"

"How are you going to get that info?"

"Hey, man. You got your skills, I got mine."

I turn to Nate and say, "Is he always like this?"

Ty answers for Nate by saying, "Like what? I told you I'd get you some info."

"I need to know how, or I'm walking away from this."

"Damn, man. My skinny ass gonna break in and snap some photos, a'ight?"

I nod. "This Wookiee dude. Where'd you meet him?"

"I already told you, bro. We did some time together."

"Where?"

"Damn, bro. In county."

"Cook County?"

"Yeah."

"When?"

"I dunno, man. Like four years ago, I think."

"Okay. So, let's talk about gaining entry into the building. They got an alarm system?"

"They got a cheap-ass alarm, yeah. Nothing I can't defeat in seconds, bro. I've scoped all that out. They don't even have motion detectors. There's a door sensor on the main door, and one on the garage bay. No problem."

"What about cameras?"

"A couple. Easy to beat."

"I don't like cameras. These days, they're small, and when they detect the slightest bit of motion, they start livestreaming everything right to people's cell phones. That happens here and we'll be facing down a group of trigger-happy cops with plenty of excuses to kill us."

"Like I said, bro. I got some skills too. There ain't a building out there I can't gain entry to, no security system I can't get around. And cameras? C'mon, bro. I got so many ways of disabling cameras it ain't even funny."

"Yeah? Okay. Get me whatever info you can on the safe then."

Nate looks at me and says, "That mean you're in, dog?"

"It means I'm closer. There's a lot more I need to know, but for now, let's find out what kind of safe I'm dealing with, and we'll go from there."

Thirty-seven days. I did the simple math and in just thirty-seven days, I'll no longer be on paper. My life will be mine again. I could quit my shitty job. No more check-ins. No more pissing into cups for random drug tests. All of it goes away in thirty-seven days.

Unless I fuck up before then.

That could be something as simple as missing a shift at work, or failing to check in, or it could be something like getting arrested for breaking into a safe that belongs to a bunch of cops.

I've got every reason to call Nate and tell him to find someone else. I've also got eighty to ninety thousand reasons to tell Nate I'm in.

The cash would come in handy. I could move out of my shithole apartment. I wouldn't need my shitty job either. People always tell you to just get another job if you hate the one you're in, but it's never that simple. It's even less simple as a convict. The truth is, I'm a thief, and that's all I'll ever be.

Everything I need is in the trunk of Nate's car. A drill and a rig. Titanium and carbide bits. A borescope. Plus some goggles, gloves, and an assortment of other tools, like screwdrivers and pliers.

Nate's parked down the street, about two blocks from the auto detailing shop. His car is the only vehicle we'll use, and when we're done, he'll drive the tools and the cash to a house in Avondale—some little place Ty has rented in his brother's name. That's where we'll all meet afterward. Ty's taking the bus, and I'm taking a blue line train. That way, we're not together and there should be nothing suspicious about us—no reason for cops to stop us and ask any questions. Just three regular blue-collar dudes commuting separately into the city for work in the early morning hours of another boring Thursday.

If all goes as planned, we'll drop the cash and equipment in Nate's trunk, he'll head to the safe house, Ty and I will hop on public transportation, and we'll all meet up at the house within an hour or so. Sure, that means Nate will be alone with about ninety grand, but we chose Nate because he's someone we both know and trust. At least I hope I can trust him. I'd hate to spend the rest of my days hunting him down.

I don't trust Ty, but he did come through with some decent photos of the safe, and thanks to some easy-to-purchase friends in the industry and some info from the dark web, I've got a pretty good idea what I'm working with.

The safe isn't high end, but the steel is a thick gauge, and it's got some anti-theft measures. Nothing I can't work around, but I've got to use caution. It's got a glass relocker, so if I get careless and drill in the wrong place, or drill too deep in the right place, the glass breaks and a massive spring-loaded bolt shoots into place, basically ensuring I won't be able to enter through the door. I could still cut through the side, but that could take hours and there's a chance I could destroy the cash inside, so I prefer the door.

Nate texts us to let us know he hasn't seen any movement in or out of the auto shop since around 3 a.m., so I give Ty the cue to disable the cameras and alarm system.

It doesn't take him long to get us inside. He's been in and out a few times this week getting me info on the safe, so he's gotten fast at it. Nate will stay in the car; be our eyes outside while I go to work.

I grab my stuff from the trunk of Nate's car. Ty holds the door for me, and I maneuver the large duffle past him, then head straight to the corner of the room where the safe awaits me.

Settling in to do my thing, I take a few measurements and mount the rig on the door, set the drill, and start making a pilot hole. It goes fast until I hit the hardplate, but that's expected, so I switch bits and start drilling into the hardplate.

Ty paces back and forth behind me. "Shit is loud, bro."

I ignore him. I told him this wouldn't be quiet, and the more I respond to his complaints, the more it slows me down.

Returning all my attention to getting through the hardplate, I settle in and let the drill get back to work. It's getting through, but it's a slow process.

Ty continues to pace behind me. I'd tell him to wait outside, but I know he'd be suspicious, likely thinking I want an opportunity to pocket some cash without him in the room. I'd assume that of him if our roles were reversed.

The drill finally breaks through, and best I can tell I didn't trigger the relocker.

Nate calls.

I flip open the buzzing phone and put it to my ear. "Yeah?"

"We got company. A black sedan and a silver two-door pulling into the parking lot."

I hang up and start shoving all my gear back into the bag.

Ty notices and says, "What's the problem?"

"Someone's here. We've gotta hide."

We've planned for this, but it's not ideal. Ty hurries toward the storeroom door. He opens it, holds it for me. I remove the drill rig and drop it into the bag, then kick a pile of metal shavings aside. There's no good way to hide the mess the drill has made though.

I join Ty in the small storage space filled with janitorial supplies. We can't see much of what's going on in the main room, our view filtered through the slats of a vent in the door.

I reach for the nine-mill stored in my waistband. Ty reaches behind his back, produces a revolver. Two convicted felons stuffed into a closet, each gripping a two- to ten-year sentence in our hands. I came prepared though. I figure if someone's keeping ninety grand inside an auto detail shop, they're more than willing to shoot anyone who tries to take it from them. Looks like Ty had the same thought.

My biggest concern right now is who's in the building, and how long they'll be here. If they go near the safe, they'll surely notice the drilled hole or the shavings on the floor.

Peering through the slats, I see nothing. No sign of anyone, and then my phone buzzes. It's Nate texting to say we're clear.

I step out of the closet and call him. "You sure we're good?"

"Yeah, dog. They were just customers. Dropped off the silver car and left the keys in some kind of overnight box. Both men left in the sedan."

"At nearly four in the goddamned morning?"

He chuckles. "You about done?"

"Hard to say."

"A'ight, I'll let you get back to it."

I tell Ty what Nate said, then drag the bag over to the safe, grab my borescope, and take a peek inside to see if I've gotten to the lock yet.

Ty's impatience grows. "Shit, man. We done yet?"

Peering down the borescope I say, "Getting there. Looks like I made it to the lock."

"So? What now?"

"Now I've got to get the fence to fall."

"Huh?"

"Basically, I've got to align things just right, so the lock disengages the bolt."

"How long's that gonna take?"

"Hard to say. Ten, twenty minutes, if we're lucky."

Ty paces again, like an animal in a zoo. I go back to work, try to focus, but dude's making me nervous, making me rethink taking this job. He also has me thinking how there'd better be cash inside this thing, and how it'd better be a lot.

Ty stares at his phone, texting someone. He paces in between sending messages and getting replies. Whoever he's chatting with has his full attention, so I don't interrupt him to open this thing, I just grab hold of the handle and give it a good thrust.

The door swings open.

Wookiee, despite his stupid name, was spot on about cash being inside. And there's a lot of it. Stacks and stacks, each wrapped with a rubber band. I'm in disbelief, honestly. I half-expected to get this thing open and find fifty bucks and some useless paperwork.

I shoot Nate a text letting him know we'll be out soon.

Ty notices the open door, and the cash inside. "Holy shit!"

Grabbing an empty duffle, I start scooping stacks of cash off a shelf and into the bag. Ty follows my lead.

I carry the tools. Ty carries the cash. Each of us drag a duffle through the disarmed door and into the parking lot where Nate's waiting in the car with the trunk lid open. We toss the bags in, and I close the trunk lid, give it a couple slaps to let Nate know we're good.

Nate takes off down the road. I set out on foot toward a blue line station. Ty walks the other direction toward a bus stop.

In about forty-five minutes, we'll all be in Avondale, where the real danger awaits.

I rise from the depths of the Belmont station and set out on foot toward the house. Nate should be there already.

The house isn't too far from the station; a few blocks east, situated practically underneath the Kennedy Expressway.

Nate's car is parked in the alleyway behind the house. I walk up to the screened porch and pull on the wooden door, drawing it back until the spring-loaded hinge stretches as far as it'll extend.

I let go.

The sound of the slamming door echoes through the neighborhood.

I head around the other side of the house and step through the front door, into the living room. A tall guy approaches from the back of the house, where I'm sure he'd been investigating the noise the screen door made as it slammed shut. I assume he's the guy they call Wookiee, but I don't wait for an introduction. Instead, I aim at him and fire off a couple quick rounds.

He drops to the ground. The semi-auto from his right hand falls beside him. I kick it away and put one more round in him, just to be sure.

Checking the other rooms, I'm hopeful that Nate was smart enough to figure out that Wookiee would be here—and that he and Ty plan to kill both of us and take the cash—but as I get to the kitchen, I find Nate dead, shot in the back several times.

I had suspicions about Ty and Wookiee early on, especially since Ty couldn't answer some very basic questions. When I asked around, no one I talked to knew anyone named Wookiee, especially not a Wookiee who'd had a stay at the Cook County jail within the past few years, like Ty claimed. County lockups are like small towns. Even in a place as busy as the Cook County jail, everybody knows everybody. The same people are in and out all the time, and with a name like Wookiee, someone would have remembered him.

I check Wookiee's pockets and find a cell phone. A quick glance at recent messages shows he's been in contact with Ty all night. HEY HOMIE YOU ABOUT DONE? one message reads. I'M HEADIN TO DA HOUSE, he said in another. Then: ILL TAKE CARE OF THAT LIL BITCH AT DA HOUSE.

In his back pocket I find a wallet. I pocket the cash, about thirty bucks, and digging through the rest, I find the typical shit, credit cards, an insurance card, punch cards from sandwich shops, and then, as expected, proof he's a cop: a membership card for the police union.

Wookiee's knowledge of the cash tipped me off. No group of cops is going to allow a former convict into their backroom poker game, and even if they did, they're not going to show off nearly a hundred grand in cash while he's there. But a rogue cop who's planning on ripping off his fellow officers? Well, I guess he turns to ex-cons like Ty for help.

From the start I've doubted Ty's skills. Sure, maybe he does know his way around alarm systems and can enter the auto shop whenever he wants, or maybe a cop buddy gave him the code to disable the alarm. I'd been suspicious of him from the start, but when he offered to give me a seventy five percent cut, that's when I knew he planned to use me, then put a bullet in me. No thief is altruistic, and no thief wants to share their earnings.

Wookiee's phone chimes. It's a text from Ty. YOU TAKE CARE OF BOTH OF THEM?

I type: YEAH HOMIE WE GOOD.

I return to Nate's body and fish the car keys out of his pocket, then head to the darkened hallway. It's near the middle of the house and has a good view of both entry points.

The front door opens and Ty swaggers in, smile on his face. "Hell yeah, bro. We did it."

He spots Wookiee's body and stops smiling.

I step out of the hallway, gun aimed at his chest.

He steps back and says, "What's this shit?"

I put two rounds in his heart.

He drops to the floor.

I put one more round in him, just to be sure.

It's hard to believe he'd been too stupid to see this

would happen either way—that even if things had gone the way he'd planned, Wookiee would have killed him anyway.

Stepping onto the porch, the roar of the nearby expressway soothes me. Hopefully folks around here are used to loud noises and haven't called the cops.

I check the trunk. It's all there. My gear. The cash. I'll have to count it later, once some dust settles. For now, I start the car and drive down the alley. Tonight, I'm splurging on a room at a hotel. One with good plumbing.

LEAKY PIPE

Sammy wags a finger at the bartender who fills the glass with another two ounces of whiskey. A house pour, nothing fancy.

Sammy's eyes stay fixed on the TV mounted to the brick wall behind the bar.

Looking up at the TV, the bartender says, "Crazy shit, eh? They're saying the gunman was a thirteen-year-old student at the school."

The sound is off, or maybe just drowned out by the music and chatter in the bar, but the closed captioning flashes across the bottom of the screen.

Sammy's been watching all morning. The disquieting details trickle in with each breaking news alert. Three killed, all boys. Shot to death in the locker room of their middle school gymnasium. Four other boys wounded, all taken to area hospitals.

At a home in the shooter's neighborhood north of Milwaukee, they found two more bodies. Children's bodies. A boy and a girl, both dead from apparent gunshot wounds. Neighbors said the two kids typically walked to school with the accused teen shooter.

The bartender leans a hip against the bar top and says, "You got kids?"

Sammy shakes his head, then sips his whiskey.

The bartender sets the bottle on the shelf behind him, then turns toward Sammy to say, "Me, neither. My brother, he's got two about that age out in Waukesha. His wife started home-schooling 'em about a year ago. Partially 'cause of shit like this."

Sammy sips his whiskey, stares at the TV.

The bartender says, "I thought it was all bullshit at the time—that home-schooling stuff. Kids at home all day, no real teachers, no interaction with other kids. But now, I'm glad she does it."

Tossing back the last drop, Sammy sets the glass on the bar and taps the rim with his finger.

"Another?"

Sammy nods.

The bartender shrugs, reaches for the bottle. "You're the boss."

He pours as the breaking news graphic fills the screen once again. One of the wounded boys has died at a hospital.

The bartender sets the bottle down, shakes his head slowly from side to side. "Horrific. That's what now? Six dead?"

Sammy nods, sips.

The bartender rests the bottle on the bar top, then says, "I think they have the shooter in custody, don't they? I think I saw that go by a little bit ago."

Sammy sips, nods. "Nabbed him early on. Caught up with him just outside the gym."

"That's some good news at least. Who is it?"

Sammy sips, shakes his head. "They haven't given the name."

"Well, I'm glad they took him alive. Maybe now we'll learn why he did this. Maybe they can find out how in the hell a thirteen-year-old kid gets hold of a semi-auto handgun and that much ammo. They said he had several extended magazines too. No kid needs to have access to shit like that. I'm sorry, but that's just how I feel about it. I know there are people who are responsible with their guns, but not all of 'em, you know? Look at this. This kid never should have had the chance to touch weaponry like that."

Sammy sips.

Holding the bottle up, the bartender says, "Another?"

Sammy shakes his head, tosses a Jackson and Hamilton on the bar top. "I'll settle up."

"You're the boss." The bartender sweeps up the bills. "I'll grab your change."

Sammy tosses back the last drop, then says, "Keep it."

"Appreciate you, boss. Be safe out there."

Sammy nods, zips up his jacket, leaves while he's still able to drive. His stomach is one big knot though. The booze is just making things worse.

Hands in the pockets of his jacket, Sammy steps out of the bar, turns the corner, walks along the stone building. The fall breeze brushes across his face.

His car is a half block down the street, parked under a tree in front of a little white bungalow. The door creaks as he opens it. He plops into the seat, rolls the window down with the hand crank, turns the key, holds it as the starter struggles. But in seconds, the motor roars to life and the radio blares.

Sammy reaches for the knob, turns the noise down, leans back in the seat. Fresh air seeps in through the window, mixes with the mustiness of the old interior.

His stomach twists. He's not sure where to go, what to do next. It's just a feeling right now. A bad gut feeling. He knows what's coming though. His gut is rarely wrong.

The kid... It's got to be him and it's just a matter of time before they name him, splash his picture all over the place. It's got to be the same kid—the one he met out by Bradford Beach last week. Noah. The lanky kid with an acne problem and braces. The one with the prepubescent voice and jittery movements.

Sammy didn't know anything about the kid when he called. The kid said he'd gotten the number from a source Sammy trusted, and so, he arranged a meet. The little shit never mentioned anything that made Sammy think he was planning something like this—that he'd end up gunning down friends and classmates.

Sammy's been in the game a long time, long enough to know not to ask customers any questions. A colleague did that once. Asked too many questions; knew too much. He was sent to prison after prosecutors proved he knew that the guy he sold a gun to was planning to kill someone with it. You can't know if you don't ask. Plausible deniability, an asset in this business.

Sammy wasn't about to make that mistake, so when the kid said he wanted a nine-millimeter, Sammy got him one. The kid had cash. Too much of it, and he didn't seem to know what he was buying—didn't seem to know what it was worth—so Sammy sold it to him: a basic little Hi-Point C9 Luger. Got nearly three times what he usually got for the same gun.

They met in the beach parking lot. The kid was sitting on one of the nearby picnic tables, his ass on the table, his feet on the bench, a backpack beside him. Dressed in blue jeans and a green Packers hoodie, just like he said he would be, the kid sat hunched over, his hands in the pocket of the hoodie.

Kid didn't hesitate when Sammy pulled into a spot close to him though. He walked over to Sammy's car with swag, got right in the passenger seat. Seemed like he'd done it before.

He had cash—a wad of it. He kept it low, out of view from walkers and joggers. He slid it to Sammy across the center console, then inspected the gun a little. Held it, bounced it up and down like the weight mattered to him, then slid it into the backpack with the extra magazines and the boxes of ammo.

He said it met his needs. He was happy, so Sammy pocketed the cash, and the kid walked away, back toward the beach.

The kid said he needed protection, and Sammy is in the business of selling protection. Simple as that. But this—what happened this morning—this shouldn't have happened.

Sammy turns up the radio for the bottom of the hour news update. The name is out there now: Noah King. Noah, the jittery kid with acne. The kid with the braces and high-pitched voice.

The news report drones on about the nice Shorewood neighborhood he lived in, its tree-lined streets, Noah's affluent family. They've already got reporters digging through his social media accounts, knocking on neighbor's doors, talking to people who knew him.

No doubt the kid is sitting in an interrogation room right now, detectives hammering him with questions, lying to him, threatening him, making him phony promises. Working to convince him they're trying to help him.

The kid will crack. No way he's prepared for what's coming. No way he's smart enough to shut his mouth and ask for a lawyer. Before long, he'll tell them where he got the gun. He'll give them Sammy's name. Kid's probably even got Sammy's number saved in his phone, and it won't be long until the cops have a warrant to search the phone, if they don't already.

It's time to get out of town, let shit blow over a little. Sammy's cousin has a cabin up north. Actually, it belongs to the family of his cousin's wife, which is even better.

Less reason anyone would think to look for him there. He stayed there once—a couple summers ago. They have a keypad lock on the front door making it easy to get in, provided the code hasn't changed. Even if it has, it's October. No one's gonna be around to hear him break a window. He can lay low there, hide out, figure out what to do next.

"Sammy." The deep voice shakes him from his reverie. His hand slides to the stock of the Smith & Wesson snub clipped to his belt as he turns his head to see who's outside his car.

It's Devin, one of his boss' lackeys. Devin's got a pistol in his hand, low and inconspicuous. A subtle threat. Isaac, another lackey, stands on the other side of the car, armed as well. No chance to draw the .38 now. Sammy'd be dead before it was out of the holster.

Devin reaches through the window, switches off the ignition, takes the keys. "Boss needs to talk to you."

"Right now?"

Devin nods.

"He in town?"

Devin nods again. "C'mon. He's waiting."

Nick is the boss. He runs the business from Chicago. Sammy takes care of the north for him. Wisconsin, parts of Minnesota. Territories that aren't as lucrative as what Nick oversees. Territories Nick isn't usually interested in. If Nick's come north, that's bad for Sammy.

Devin opens the car door for him. Waits. Sammy slides out, but before his feet are even set beneath him, Devin's taking the .38 from his belt. Isaac steps in, pats him down, checks for a leg piece. Sammy's only carrying the .38, but it belongs to Devin now.

With a firm grip on his elbow, Devin coaxes him toward the black SUV parked across the street. Issac opens the back door and Sammy climbs into the back seat. Before he can settle in, Devin slides in next to him and Isaac climbs into the driver seat, pulls away from the curb at a jolting speed.

Sammy stares out the window; a blur of homes and businesses pass along Center Street as they cross over I-43. Issac makes a turn, south on MLK.

Sammy's got questions, but Devin's not the type to answer them, even if he were to ask.

Nick's pissed, of course he is. All of this is bad for him, and bad for business. The kid—the goddamned kid. Noah. When he called, he said he was being bullied and needed protection.

This business is a tricky one. A delicate balance between connecting customers with what they need while staying out of their shit. A business where emotions can't be involved. It's a simple business: a customer hands over cash, Sammy hands over a gun. It doesn't matter why the customer needs or wants protection. It's about providing a service, getting referrals.

Isaac makes a couple quick turns into an industrial area, a part of town Sammy's never seen. The buildings outside pass in a blur.

Most customers understand the boundaries. But not this kid—not Noah. From the start, he offered Sammy way too much information. He said some bullies had jumped him. They'd beaten him and kicked him while he was on the ground, cracked some ribs. They'd been tormenting him since the start of the school year, he said.

These were details Sammy didn't ask for, but they were things he understood. Things he'd experienced. Things he'd wished he could have put a stop to when he was Noah's age. And so, by the time he was in that parking lot with Noah, he felt like he was helping the kid. He'd let emotion enter the deal, and now he was paying the price.

Issac makes another turn, tossing Sammy into the door of the SUV. Sammy struggles back to his seat just as Issac pulls into a vacant lot next to an old warehouse. A huge two-story red brick building that's been long forgotten, neglected. Most of the windows have been busted out, others are boarded up.

Isaac parks in the gravel lot. Devin slides out, waits for Sammy to follow.

Again with a tight grip on his elbow, Devin leads him to a side entrance of the massive building, a large wooden door, its white paint faded and peeling.

The interior of the decaying structure is just as uninspiring as the outside. A drab hallway with threadbare commercial carpeting that's curling away at the edges along the walls, exposing the water-damaged wood beneath. A musty smell assaults Sammy's nose, the dampness settles on his tongue.

"Wait in here." Devin directs him into an office at the end of the hallway. A small, windowless space long since emptied of its furnishings except for a tattered office chair in the corner. The room is humid, dank. The stench of something floats in the air. A dead possum, maybe? Rotting mice, perhaps?

Sammy stands in the center of the room, examines the situation. There's one way in, and out. No one knows he's here.

The door thuds as it closes behind him.

Sammy's alone.

He takes a lap. Concrete block walls, rotting wood floors, a drop ceiling covered in water-stained tiles. In the corner, a constant drip from a pipe above, the droplets hit the water that's pooled on the damp wood below. The sound is rhythmic.

Drip. Drip-drip. Drip. Drip-drip-drip.

The beat repeats, uninterrupted and Sammy takes a second lap. Nothing's changed. Pulling the well-used office chair from the corner, he turns it, inspects it, takes a seat. It sits low, the lift mechanism too worn to support his weight.

Nick doesn't come to town often. The fact that this visit coincides with what happened at that school can't be coincidental. Nick is here because of Noah. Nick is here because of Sammy.

Sammy sits, stares at the gray wall.

Drip. Drip-drip. Drip. Drip-drip-drip.

Of course Nick's not happy that one of their guns was used. It's going to draw attention to them. And to Sammy, for sure. By now, the cops may already have his name. They could even be seeking a search warrant for his apartment.

Drip. Drip-drip. Drip.

Nick can help though. He's got connections all over, even as far as Mexico. Maybe he's got a place Sammy could use for a few weeks. Maybe even something on a beach. Lay low, get some sun, drink some colorful cocktails. Shit will blow over, then Sammy can get back to it.

Things here will be intense for a while though. Cops are gonna want to talk to him. Parents are going to demand that the source of the gun be brought to justice. Politicians will talk about passing stricter laws. The fervor will be loud; the community's anger and outrage will be heard across the country. All of it will tamp down once the next mass shooting happens, or maybe even when the first major winter storm hits.

Drip. Drip-drip.

Like a leaky pipe, the water will eventually drain, and the damage will be forgotten.

Drip.

The door creaks open. Nick walks in, flanked by his goons. Sammy stands, but Nick waves his hand and says, "Please. Sit."

Sammy complies, lowering himself back into the chair once again.

Nick paces in front of him. Devin and Isaac stand guard at the door.

Back and forth, Nick paces in silence, so Sammy says, "I'm surprised to see you."

Nick stops, stares at Sammy. "Yeah? Did you hear about the shooting?"

Sammy nods. "I'm sorry. I know it's bad for business. I had no idea the kid was thinking about anything like this, I swear."

Nick is silent. Only stares, so Sammy says, "The kid told me he'd been attacked by some jocks at school. Said it happened a bunch of times and that he wanted some protection from them. That's all he said. I didn't know he was gonna do something like this."

Still, Nick stares.

Shifting in the uncomfortable chair, Sammy says, "You gotta believe me. I had no idea what he was planning. Shit never even crossed my mind. He said he needed it for protection, and he was willing to pay— pay way more than he shoulda—so I sold it to him. I didn't know what he'd do, I swear. I didn't know this would happen."

Nick paces again. "But it did happen, Sammy."

"I know, and I'm sorry. Shit'll blow over though, right? It always does. Maybe business takes a hit for a few months, but it'll blow over. I'm willing to lower my fee until it does, you know? Help make up for any financial losses you incur from this."

Nick paces—walking slowly from the doorway to the wall, then back again. He stops in the center of the room, looks at Sammy and says, "Six dead."

"God. I know. I saw."

"Five boys, one little girl."

"I know. I heard. Like I said, I didn't know what the little shit was planning. I had no idea. I wouldn't have sold to him if I did, you know that, right?"

Nick stares. "Do you know the name of the little girl?"

Sammy shakes his head. "They haven't released the names of the victims. Not that I've heard anyway."

"Her name's Lauren. Lauren Alfano." Nick paces, says, "She was only twelve."

"Shit. That's messed up."

Nick nods. "Yes. It is. She was in band. First chair flute. Good grades. Wanted to be a doctor someday." He smirks. "Ambitious, I know. Doesn't mean she would have followed through, but I admire the loftiness of the goal. How about you, Sammy? Do you admire her ambition?"

He nods. "Ye—yeah. I do."

"Well, either way, one thing that we know with absolute certainty is that little Lauren will never be a doctor. Or anything else, for that matter, isn't that right?"

Sammy nods. "It's—it's fucked up."

"Yes. Yes, it is." Nick paces. "What's his name? The killer?"

"Noah."

"Right." Nick nods. "Noah King. Did you know that monster shot Lauren three times?"

"God, no. I—I haven't heard any of the details."

"Three times, Sammy. Once in the back of the head. The round exited through her face."

Sammy's stomach tightens. "Jesus. That's seriously messed up. I—I had no idea."

"She was a friend of his. They were neighbors. They'd grown up together. Played together. Yet, this monster put a gun to the back of her head and pulled the trigger. Point blank, Sammy. The exit wound ripped apart her beautiful face."

"God." Sammy's squirms in the chair. "That's grotesque. I had no idea what he was planning. I swear to you, Nick. You believe me, don't you?"

"I agree." Nick nods. "It is grotesque. That's a good word for it."

"I—I swear I had no idea that he was planning any of this."

Her family isn't going to be able to see her again, not even in a casket. Do you have any idea what kind of damage is caused to someone's face when something like that happens?"

The contents of Sammy's stomach shift. The whiskey bubbles. He swallows it down and says, "God. That's so messed up."

"Yes, it is. She was a brilliant, beautiful little girl. My sister's kid. And to think, she'd moved her family up here for a quieter, safer life."

"Oh, shit. Nick, I—I'm so sorry. I didn't know she was family. You know that, right? I didn't know any of this would happen. I didn't know he was going to kill kids, and I especially didn't know who he was going after."

"Sure, I understand. Cost of doing business. Collateral damage, right? In this business of ours, now and then, our product is bound to wind up on the evening news in tragic ways."

Nick walks toward Issac, takes the nine millimeter from his hand.

The gun at his side, Nick says, "Today's tragic news is that my niece took three nine millimeter bullets simply because she'd associated with the wrong kid."

Sammy shifts in the chair, sitting up straighter. "Nick, I'm sorry. I—I didn't know what he'd do. I don't know what else to say. Please, just give me a chance to make up for this. Please?"

Nick raises the gun, points it at Sammy. "That doesn't undo any of the damage, does it?"

"Nick, please, man. I am so sorry. I don't know what else to say. What can I do to show you how sorry I am? Please, just give me a chance. Let me do something to help, or to make up for this."

Nick's finger moves to the trigger as he steps behind Sammy, the barrel of the gun inches from the back of his skull. Sammy pleads again, but he knows what's coming, knows what Nick has to do. Simply because he associated with the wrong kid.

I LIKE YOU, YOU SEEM NICE

The sun fades in the distance as she searches for Betty Lou, the six-year-old terrier-poodle mix who's been with her through four moves and too many bad relationships to count.

The streets empty of people on the cool autumn night, she wanders the neighborhood that's still new to her, hoping to be reunited with the best companion she's ever known.

"Betty Lou? Here girl!"

She'd gotten her from a rescue five years ago, though Betty Lou had come with the name Madison. The name didn't fit Betty Lou's personality at all, and it was also the name of her worst enemy from high school, so she had to rename the dog.

The neighborhood streets in near darkness, her path is lit only by the occasional streetlamp.

She whistles for the dog. "Betty Lou? Betty Lou? Here girl!"

Her friend Julia once pointed out that Madison was one of the Founding Fathers and joked that if she were to adopt a dog named after a rebel, she'd better be prepared for a lifetime of rebellious behavior. This played a role in the decision to rename the dog, but now, as she wanders the darkening streets dressed only in plaid-print pajamas and flip-flops, she couldn't help but notice that no matter her name, the dog was a rebel, always in search of freedom.

Betty Lou had escaped from every house they'd called home; however, at the new house, Betty Lou had figured out how to escape in record time. Tonight was her third successful escape in the four months they'd lived in Denver.

The first escape happened a little over a week ago. After a long day of work, while doing dishes and mindlessly staring out the window, she watched with faint wonderment as Betty Lou effortlessly jumped onto the garbage cans stored next to the fence, balanced on them briefly, then leapt over the fence on her way to freedom. It happened so quickly and gracefully that she assumed Betty Lou had been planning the escape all day.

"Betty Lou?" She whistles again. "Come here girl!"

The second escape happened just three days ago, this time while she was at work. Betty Lou had some-how manipulated the screen in a living room window, pushing it aside before stepping out onto the deck. The deck led to the yard, which led to the fence, which this time, Betty Lou dug underneath, placing her once again on a path to freedom. Luckily, the woman next door found Betty Lou and kept her safe in the garage until she returned from work.

She whistles. "Here girl!"

Betty Lou replaced Cory. Cory was not a dog, not in the biological sense anyway. Cory was a boyfriend. For a time, Cory wasn't just *a* boyfriend, he was *the* boyfriend. Marriage material boyfriend. A mother-approved boyfriend. A rare find indeed.

But it's been quite some time since Cory was any of these things. Cory is gone now. Perhaps not forgotten, but gone. Replaced by Betty Lou.

Although, technically, David replaced Cory first.

David was opposite Cory in every way. Cory was a stay-at-the-office-all-night businessman; David was ex-military. Cory was short; David was tall. Cory cheated on her; David... Well, okay, they were alike in some ways.

"Betty Lou?" She whistles. "Come here!"

Turning up another unfamiliar road, her exposed feet sting, and as the cool fall air settles in, she wishes she'd thought to grab a jacket on her way out the door, along with better footwear. A flashlight would have been a good idea too. The streets are lit poorly and it's a struggle to make out objects that aren't directly under a streetlight.

Headlights from behind light up her path. The engine quiets and the car creeps closer.

Her chest tightens as she reaches to her side, but her heart pounds upon the realization that she doesn't have the small canister of pepper spray she usually takes on walks because in her hurry to find Betty Lou, she'd neglected to grab it.

Fighting an urge to turn and look at the car, she keeps walking, her head low. At the end of the street sits a fire station. She could seek help there, but it's several blocks away.

At the intersection, the car slows to a stop. Without looking at it, she turns the corner, walks away from the car. Her head down, she powers forward.

The car accelerates again, but it goes straight.

She turns her head, sneaks a glimpse of it. It's a nice-looking car. Metallic silver. New looking. European. Probably expensive.

She whistles. "Betty Lou?"

Betty Lou offered a good distraction from Cory. And from David. And from Sam. And even from Kevin, the guy she most recently moved on from.

So far, Kevin had proven harder to forget than the others though. She couldn't pinpoint why exactly. He wasn't as good looking as the other guys. He didn't have the best job. He wasn't funny or particularly nice, but still, he stuck in her memories the most, maybe simply because he'd been the most recent.

Julia had told her to move on, to forget about him. "You'll meet someone new," she added.

It was laughable advice. The concept of moving on probably seemed easy for people like Jennifer. She hadn't had to move on since roughly the third week of the ninth grade because she married her high school sweetheart and they've been blissfully married for more than ten years now.

As for meeting someone new, well, sure. That was exactly how things work. Either you met someone new, or you died old and alone.

"Betty Lou? Here girl!"

Moving on from Kevin was tough though. He was the one who decided they weren't working out. He didn't know how to handle her, he said. Apparently she was too "intense" at times, at least that's what he'd screamed at her one night. So, he's gone now. She was better off without him anyway. He couldn't handle things, now he's gone, and she still has Betty Lou.

Or at least she had her.

"Betty Lou? Where the hell are you? Come here girl!"

She liked the *idea* of Kevin better than she actually liked Kevin anyway. Being with Kevin meant she would never again have to move on or meet someone new. Or die alone.

Meeting people was not easy, and now she was getting too old for the bar and club scene. At least she thought so. And even if she did decide to bury her self-respect and dig out her clubwear from the depths of her closet, she'd have no one to go with since all her close friends were married or in serious relationships.

Julia insisted that dating apps were the modern equivalent of singles bars. Reluctantly, she'd tried a few, but so far, she'd only met total weirdos and skeezy creepers.

Headlights over the hill blind her. The same fancy silver car. She ignores it, keeps her gaze forward and it passes her.

Relief washes over her, but the car turns around. The lights behind her now, the engine quiets again as it pulls up to the curb a few feet away.

She subconsciously reaches for the pepper spray, reminded again of the massive mistake she made.

The car continues driving along the curb beside her, slowly it creeps closer, and then the tinted window lowers. "Excuse me."

It's a man's voice. She ignores it, keeps walking.

The voice gets louder. "Sorry to bother you, but I was wondering if you're all right?"

The voice sounds pleasant enough, harmless. She stops, turns to look at the man speaking to her. He's handsome. Nice eyes. Dark, fashionably styled hair. Safe to speak to, probably.

She nods. "I'm fine, thank you."

The man scans her with his eyes. "Okay. I just wanted to check." He pauses like he's going to leave, but then says, "The only reason I ask is because you seem to be in your PJs."

Her face warms. Some might think she looks like a damsel in distress, this man, however, clearly thinks she looks more like an escapee from a mental hospital. "Oh, yeah. I'm uh... I'm looking for my dog. She got out of the yard. I didn't have time to change."

The man nods like he understands, like it happens to him every day. "You must be freezing. Why don't you hop in? I'll drive you around the neighborhood."

And she was never heard from again... "No, thank you. I'm fine."

"You sure?" He pats the empty passenger seat beside him. "This baby's got heated seats."

"Thank you, but I'm fine."

"Okay." He shrugs. "Hope you find your doggie."

"Thank you."

He waits, probably hoping she'll change her mind. She starts walking, and he eventually pulls away, offering a little wave out the window as he passes.

Neither Cory nor David would ever have offered that kind of assistance.

Sam might have.

Kevin definitely wouldn't have.

He was the most selfish of the bunch, selfish in most every way imaginable. They always dined where *he* wanted to dine. Watched movies *he* wanted to watch. And in the bedroom, it was all about Kevin too. If he wanted sex, she was expected to provide it. If she wanted sex and he wasn't in the mood, they didn't have sex. And no matter what, she was always on top, always doing the work, and she always went down on him. He never reciprocated. Not one damn time.

Kevin could be adventurous at times though. He liked occasional role play, and the handcuffs... They were his idea entirely. She'd never suggested them; never mentioned them at all. Kevin just came home from work one day with a pair. He walked in from the garage, smiled, and dangled them from his pointer finger.

The sight of the handcuffs brought back a torrent of memories—memories of Cory, David, and of Sam, and all the fun she'd had with them.

With Cory, she had to push the subject. She'd been the one to buy the handcuffs, and she'd been the one to suggest she cuff him to the bed frame. It took some convincing, but she got him to agree.

David had a pair of handcuffs from a stint he did as a security guard after leaving the service. He liked the idea when she suggested it but wanted to chain her to the headboard and do god-knows-what to her. It took a little convincing, and a little trickery, but by the end of the night, she had him chained to the bed.

Sam was a lot easier. By the time Sam came along, she'd mastered her understanding of how men's minds worked; how easy it was to get them to do things with even the slightest hint that the night would end with sex. She felt stupid, looking back. She'd wasted so much energy on Cory and on David when all she would have had to do was give them a pair of handcuffs, flash a little tit, and tell them what to do.

"Betty Lou? Here girl."

A smile creeps across her face as she thinks about those men, and all men, amused by how upset guys got when they had to cede power to her.

It was fun too, how squirmy they got when she'd secure their hands to the bed frame, and how worried they seemed as she brought out the rope and tied up each leg. The look of confusion as she wrapped the mattress beneath them with plastic. The look of terror the moment they spotted the knife in her hand. The discomposed sounds of agony that tended to erupt from the mouths of burly men as she slid the knife between their ribs. The feeling of flesh slicing, of muscle ripping.

The headlights again blind her, the car pulls toward the curb, slows. The engine quiets.

She stops, turns to look at the car, crosses her arms.

The passenger window lowers, and Betty Lou's happy, dumb face pops out.

The man leans over. "Looking for this little one?"

"Yes!" She rushes toward the car. "Where did you find her?"

"Over on Vine. She was in someone's yard, rummaging through a garbage can that'd been knocked over."

"Thank you so much for finding her. Sorry if she caused you any trouble."

"No trouble at all. My name's Christian, by the way."

"Hi. I'm, um... Madison."

"It's nice to meet you, Madison. Now, c'mon. Hop in. I'll give you both a ride home."

"Oh, no thank you. We can walk."

"C'mon. Let me do this for you. It's only getting colder, and darker, and this little furry one is already settled in."

She looks up the street as she contemplates the offer. She's a good mile from home. Betty Lou seems comfortable in the car, and Christian, well, Christian seems pleased to be a knight in shining armor. And given that he's fallen for the lost dog bit so easily, it would be fun to see how the rest went.

She nods. "Okay. Thank you." She reaches for the handle, opens the door.

Betty Lou climbs into her lap and sticks her face in the breeze of the open window as Christian pulls away from the curb. "I really appreciate this."

He turns to her, smiles. "You bet. I didn't like the idea of you out here wandering the streets alone, and I'm a sucker for dogs."

A smirk slides across her face. "That's sweet. I'm new to the area, and Betty Lou here is new to the area too. I haven't figured out how to keep her confined to the yard yet."

"She's a terrier, right?"

"Part terrier. Part terror too."

He laughs. It's a staged laugh. He too is playing a role.

He pats Betty Lou on the head. "Terriers are tough to contain. We had a couple when I was growing up, and they were always getting out of the yard."

She smiles a fake smile. Thanks him again for the ride, for saving her, for being there when she needed him most. All the things he wants to hear.

She directs him down the street, then a left, then a right, directs him three blocks up Gaylord to the little brick bungalow on the right.

Christian follows direction nicely.

He makes his move as they near the house, compliments her, tells her she's pretty. She knows it's a line. Her hair up in a simple chignon, basically no makeup on her face—he doesn't care if she's pretty. If sex is a remote possibility, he figures it's worth a shot, just like every man.

"Thank you, but I'm a mess."

He stops in front of the house, turns, smiles. "I very much disagree."

She looks toward the house, then back at Christian. "Um... You're welcome to come in for a glass of wine, if you'd like."

"Yeah?" A smile involuntarily encompasses his entire face. "Okay. I'd like that."

She carries Betty Lou inside, sets her down, then disarms the alarm system. Christian walks in behind her, begins inspecting the living room, inspecting her artwork and nicknacks.

She kicks off her flip-flops. "Don't judge. I'm still not unpacked."

"The place looks great."

"Well, thank you for saying that. It's just a rental, until I get settled." She motions toward the sofa. "Make yourself comfortable."

Christian nods, sits down.

"I'll get us something to drink."

He crosses his legs, drapes one over the other, extends his arm across the back of the sofa. "Mind if I ask where you moved here from?"

Stepping into the kitchen, she shouts over her shoulder. "Saint Louis." Reaching up her neck, she unclips her hair, lets it drop to her shoulders, combs it out with her fingers.

"What brings you to Denver?"

Glancing at the knife block on her counter, she pulls out the chef's knife, runs her finger across the top. "I needed a change, I guess you could say. Too many... ghosts behind me."

"I hear that."

Returning the knife to the block, she unbuttons her top, allowing it to flow open. "How about you? Lived here long?"

"Most of my life. Went away to college for a few years, but only to Boulder, so not far at all." He chuckles. "How about you? Did you go to school out in Missouri?"

She steps into the doorway, leans against the wall at an angle to allow her top to flop open and show the flesh of her flat tummy. "I'm afraid I don't have any wine, sorry."

"That's um... That's okay. I'm not all that into wine anyway."

She smiles, walks past him, toward the hallway. "Good, because I do have some other ideas for things to do."

She doesn't look, but he's behind her. Of course he is.

The clunk of his loafers hitting the wooden floors echoes down the hallway, the pressure of each step vibrates beneath her bare feet.

He obediently follows her into the bedroom, presumptively unbuttoning his shirt, smiling wildly.

Opening the drawer of her nightstand, she digs until she feels the cold steel. She holds the handcuffs in the air long enough for him to see them, then tosses them onto the bed.

Facing him, she runs her pointer finger down his bare chest. "Once you have these clothes off, go ahead and chain yourself to the headboard for me, okay?"

He stumbles out a response, spitting out something between a "yes" and an "okay."

She smiles, plants a light kiss on his lips. "I'm going to freshen up a bit. You'd better be where I want you when I come out."

She turns toward the hallway and walks to the bathroom where she runs a brush through her hair, then ties it behind her head, out of the way. Buttoning her top, she straightens it and leaves the room.

A peek down the hallway reveals Christian has again followed directions well. His hands cuffed to the metal headboard, he's smiling.

In the living room, she finds Betty Lou with her head resting between her paws.

From the hallway, Christian's voice calls. "Hey, um... You—you're coming back, right?"

A smirk fills her face. "Be right there."

She opens the drawer by the sink, pulls out a wad of rope and a plastic drop cloth. Stopping at the knife block, she pulls out the chef's knife, runs a finger across the steel, then tucks it under her arm.

Betty Lou eyes her as she steps out of the kitchen.

"What?"

Her tail wags, her head raises.

"You want credit for this one?"

With a slight tilt of her head, the speed of the tail wagging increases.

"Don't pretend like you didn't have fun exploring the neighborhood."

A bark, once single yap, reverberates in the small room.

"Fine. You did good tonight, is that what you want to hear? Now, if you'll excuse me, I'm going to go have some fun of my own."

With a small moan of satisfaction, Betty Lou again positions her head contently between her paws. A deserved bit of rest after a night of hard work.

TOUGH MESSES

The house is a dump. I'm not sure what I expected. More than what I'm looking at, that's for sure. More than this old, narrow box with peeling paint and missing roof shingles.

There's no address on the building, so I pull out my phone and double check the directions Antonio gave me earlier: Green Line to Pulaski, walk down Lake two blocks, first right, then second right, second house on the right.

This has to be the place. Unless I miscounted the houses. The block only has a few. Seems like there used to be a lot more at some point, but either they burned down, or the city tore them down. Now sits a spattering of houses with a whole bunch of overgrown weeds in between them.

It's hard to believe this is Antonio's place because the dude is a huge player. You want it, Antonio's got it— or he can get it. Meth, coke, heroin, fentanyl, guns, explosives. Like I said, this dude can get you what you need. He's supposedly tied to cartel guys down south who bring shit up from Mexico. Dude must be making stacks of cash every goddamned day, so I assumed he'd have a nicer house. Shit, my apartment is nicer than this place and my apartment is a shithole.

Stepping onto the front porch, I take a deep breath. To be honest, I'm sweatin' a bit. Antonio's a big dude, and he makes me nervous as fuck. That don't make me a pussy. Everyone's nervous around Antonio. Dude is big, and dude is temperamental. One minute he's making jokes, the next he's pointing a gun in your face asking if you want to die today.

I knock.

No answer.

I hear chatter coming from a TV inside, so I knock harder.

Goddamnit, I don't want to be here. Not at all. I owe Antonio big though. He texted earlier. Told me to swing by tonight. I'm not in the position to say no, so here I am. Dude said he's got a way for me to clear my debt. Sure, I'm fucking freaked out about what that could mean, but at the same time, I ain't got another way to pay him, so here I am.

The dirty wooden door swings open. Carlos stares at me. He's Antonio's brother, or half-brother. Something like that. He's a small, wiry guy who's creepy as shit. Dude barely ever says a word, but he stares a lot.

He's staring at me now.

"Uh, is Antonio here?"

More staring.

I try again. "He told me to drop by."

Carlos backs away from the door and steps aside, giving me room to enter. At least I assume he's giving me permission to enter. If the asshole would act like a normal dude and say "come in" or something, shit would be a lot easier.

Taking the chance that I've read him right, I step inside. Without saying nothing, he closes the door behind me, then fucking stares some more.

I try again. "Is Antonio here?"

Finally the prick nods his head toward the other side of the house, giving me some form of communication. Then to my total shock, he speaks and says, "Kitchen. He'll be out soon."

Well, there ya go. *Soon.* However long that is. But at least I've got confirmation that he's here. Now if Carlos would tell me to, like, I dunno, take a seat or something, I'd be happy to wait. Instead, he stares at me some more. I don't want to look at his dumb ass too much, so I take a look around the house. The inside is as unimpressive as the outside. Worn brown carpet. A gray couch that's ratty and stained. He's got some old oak end tables, an oak coffee table, and an oak entertainment center. Sitting on the entertainment center is a small-ass flat panel TV, shoved in front of an old clunky tube TV that no one's bothered to throw out yet.

Antonio appears in the doorway from the other part of the house and says, "Rojo! You made it."

Dude insists on calling me Rojo because of the color of my hair. I've been called "Red" a shit-ton in life, so at least it's a new take on a classic.

I nod, try to act normal, then say, "Yeah. Thanks for the directions."

"Yeah, yeah. Glad you found it okay." Antonio waves his hand toward the tattered couch. "Take a seat, amigo."

I plop down on the far end, assuming he's going to sit down as well. He doesn't. Instead, he paces in front of me. He's wearing tan Dickies and a Bulls jersey, his shitty prison tats on full display down both of his pudgy arms.

Back and forth he paces, his leg brushes against the old coffee table, when he reaches the end, he spins and repeats, going the other direction.

Carlos stands to the side, hunched over the entertainment center with one arm resting on top of it. He's engrossed in something on the TV, some program in Spanish. I make out every fourth or fifth word. Seems to be some kind of soap opera.

Antonio paces but says nothing, so I say, "How long you lived in this place?"

Antonio snort-laughs. "Shit, homie. This ain't mine. Belongs to a business associate."

I'm out of things to say, so I settle on, "Cool."

"Rojo." He stops pacing and stares at me.

I await more words, but he just stares, so I say, "What's up?"

He puffs his chest and says, "You got my money, bitch?"

Goddamnit. Did he forget why he called me here? Or was this all just a setup? Some ass-backwards invite to a stomping? Like a little bitch, I trip over my words. "I um... I thought, uh, I thought you had a solution for that?"

An evil grin fills his chubby face. "Relax, homie. I'm just fucking wit' you." He chuckles darkly.

I chuckle too, sorta. It's more of a weird, nervous noise. Anxiety manifesting itself in an awkward sound that trickles out of my mouth, something I hope he doesn't pick up on.

Antonio grins again, then leans over to reach for something behind the end table. When he stands again, he's holding a black backpack. Another creepy grin fills his face as he says, "Check this out, homie. I got options for you."

He holds the backpack with his left hand as his right hand plunges inside. He pulls out a large semi-auto pistol, inspects it, waves it around, then points it at me.

I tense up. My throat tightens.

Antonio sets the gun on the coffee table. "Smith & Wesson nine-mil. Option one." His hand returns to the backpack and out comes another black handgun. He chuckles as he looks at it. "Glock 23, forty cal. Option two." He sets it on the table. "Always a good choice, right, amigo?"

I say nothing as his hand returns to the bag. He pulls out another black handgun. "HK forty-five cal. My personal favorite. A forty-five will always get the job done, homie."

I stare down at the three guns placed in a row on the coffee table. They're all nice guns. Expensive guns. Deadly guns. I just don't know what he expects me to do with them.

I look up from the table, meet his eyes. He's grinning that evil grin, which tells me nothing other than he's as fucked up as I figured.

It's quiet in the room, except for the Spanish soap opera on the TV. I ask, "So, how do we take care of my debt?"

Dude just laughs. It's a creepy laugh and it makes my asshole tighten. I have no idea what his plan is, but I'm hating it already.

He picks the HK up, pops the magazine out, then inspects the pistol. From the couch, it looks like the mag is fully loaded and I start to sweat some more. Dude can blow my head off right now and there ain't shit I can do about it. No one knows I'm here. All he'd have to do is shoot me and dump my body somewhere. No one would ever know what happened.

His cell phone rings. He flips it open and takes the call, speaking in Spanish.

Damnit, I should have paid more attention in my high school Spanish classes. School was never my thing though. I slogged through high school and came to Chicago for college. Within just a couple months I knew my ass was going to fail.

That's how I wound up in Antonio's world. It started with me buying shit from him when I was still in school. After dropping out, I started selling shit for him, mostly so I could make rent and avoid moving back in with my parents. Now, nearly two years later, here I am, sweating my balls off wondering if this insane son of a bitch is going to kill me over the few grand worth of shit he fronted me.

He flips the phone closed and returns to the edge of the coffee table. "Where were we, Rojo?"

I stare at the small collection of handguns on the table in front of me. Perhaps I could grab one, shoot Antonio, turn and shoot Carlos, then run. But where to? The train? A bus stop? Then where? At some point, one of Antonio's guys would come looking for me. Or maybe the cops find me before that. Sure, it'd be self-defense, but to get to that point in court I'd have to explain how I'd been slinging shit for Antonio for years. How I fucked up. How I owed him.

Antonio chuckles another dark laugh as he picks up the Glock.

My chance is gone. Any quick movement now and he kills me here on this shitty couch.

"You owe me, right?" He inspects the Glock. "We can fix that."

"How?"

Again he chuckles, then says, "Cash isn't the only payment I accept, homie."

I don't know if he thinks he's being clear, or if he's trying to fuck with me, but I have no idea what he's getting at. I wait for him to explain, but he just stands there, staring at me with the goddamned gun in his hand.

The silence is too awkward, so I say, "How do I make shit right?"

Another evil grin slides across his face. He seems pleased, like he's been waiting for me to ask. He sets the Glock down and says, "You're gonna take care of a problem for me. Tonight."

This gets Carlos' attention. He turns off the TV and joins us, sits on the edge of the couch, close to me—close to the guns. He picks up the HK, checks it out, sets it back on the table.

I look at Antonio and say, "So, how do I make shit right?"

Again he paces. "Someone's coming by later. A thief. Bitch took over eighty grand from me. He thinks I don't know, but I know. Tonight, you take care of him."

It hits me: I'm not here to die. I'm here to kill.

Antonio's talking, but his words aren't registering. I've never killed anyone, and I don't want to.

The TV is on again and I'm staring at an infomercial for some kind of cookware that's supposedly going to revolutionize my life. If I cooked at all, that is.

Staring at the TV, I try to focus on the stupid show, try to think about anything other than killing some dude, but I can't.

Next to me on the couch is the Smith & Wesson SD9. I chose it mostly because it's a gun I'm familiar with. My dad had a similar model, and he let me fire it a handful of times.

At paper targets.

Not people.

The guy on the TV is shouting now, his mind blown by how even burnt eggs slide right off the pan's patented non-stick coating.

Antonio and Carlos are in the kitchen packaging some baggies for a dealer to pick up. Nathan—the guy I'm supposed to kill—thinks that's what he's coming over for. Instead, Antonio wants me to shoot him. Not right away, he told me. I'm supposed to let Nathan come in, get comfortable. Bullshit a little, let him see the batch of crack Antonio and Carlos just made. Then, pop!

Antonio wants me to do it in the kitchen where the floor is covered in linoleum. He's got a couple bottles of bleach nearby, but he said someone else will take care of the cleaning. All I gotta do is take care of Nathan.

The guy on the TV is now marveling at how the pan is also dishwasher safe. He shouts, "Even tough messes are no problem!"

I've run through this particular mess in my head a lot, and it's a problem. I know Nathan. Not well, but well enough. He'll greet me with that cupped handshake thing he does to everyone and probably pull me in for a brief man-hug. He'll walk with swag to the kitchen, pretend to be impressed by what Antonio and Carlos did, and then he'll start bragging about how much of it he'll be able to move. Something like that at least.

I'm trying to get angry. Trying to find a reason the guy deserves to die. He's arrogant and kind of a douchebag, but I've got no real beef with him. Not enough to do what I'm supposed to do.

My plan is to do it from behind. It seems better if he's not looking at me, I guess. It'll be quicker for him too. Just a quick shot to the back of the head while he's bragging about some bullshit.

I've never seen nobody get shot in the head, except in movies. It seems the quickest though, and one shot should do it. Antonio wants it done in one shot. He said one shot isn't likely to attract too much attention from the neighbors.

It's almost three in the morning and the cookware infomercial is gone, replaced by ads for some miracle weight loss supplement.

Nathan was supposed to be here two hours ago. Antonio seems unbothered by this though. He's been bagging shit and taking phone calls for the past three hours. Don't seem like he's even thinking about Nathan, but that's the only thing I can think about.

I think he's got a kid, if I'm remembering right. A son, I think. The mother has custody, and I'm not sure how involved Nathan is in the kid's life, but still, dude is a fucking father to someone. Dude's parents probably care about him too. Siblings too, maybe.

"Rojo!" Antonio shouts from the kitchen. "Get your pale ass in here."

I hop up and head to the kitchen. Carlos is sitting at the table. Antonio's standing at the fridge. I look at Antonio and say, "Yeah?"

"Cerveza?"

He extends his hand toward me, and I take the beer from him. I don't really want it. My stomach is one big fucking knot, and for hours, I've felt like I might puke, but maybe the alcohol will calm me.

Antonio pops the cap off his and leans against the counter. After a swig he says, "He'll be here soon."

"Yeah? How long?"

He sips, shrugs. "Soon."

It's a meaningless measurement of time and I'm unable to wrap my mind around it.

Antonio takes another swig of beer, then says, "You got your piece?"

"It's on the couch."

"Well, you'd better go get it, homie. Unless you're ready to go old school and do this shit with your bare hands."

He laughs.

Carlos laughs.

I fumble my way back to the living room to retrieve the S&W. I set my beer on the coffee table and pick up the gun. I pop the magazine out and take a look before sliding it back in. I got no idea why. I guess because they do that shit in TV shows. I chamber a round and take a deep breath before sliding the gun into the waistband of my jeans, nestled against my back. Again, I don't know why. It's what people do, ain't it? I can't exactly be standing there with a gun in my hand when Nathan comes in.

I grab my beer and head back to the kitchen. Antonio and Carlos don't seem to notice me. I lean against the counter and slide over toward the sink, out of the way.

Soon. He'll be here *soon*. I've got to do this, *soon*.

The doorbell rings and all my muscles tighten. My neck is so stiff I can barely turn my head from side to side. Part of me hopes it ain't Nathan; part of me hopes it is so I can get this shit over with.

Antonio goes to the door. I reposition the nine-millimeter in my waistband, making sure my T-shirt covers it.

The door swings open and Nathan walks into the room. He's wearing a Bulls jersey too, like he and Antonio are in some club together.

Clasping Antonio's hand, Nathan pulls him in for a man-hug. I'm fucking frozen in the doorway to the kitchen. What do I do here? Go say hi to the dude? Wait for him to come into the kitchen?

Before I can think about it too much, he steps into the living room. Someone follows. Katy, his girlfriend. Shit.

No one said shit about no girlfriend coming with him. Maybe now Antonio will call the whole fucking thing off.

Nathan sees me and says, "Mikey, bro, what's up?" He grabs my hand, pulls me shoulder-to-shoulder as he pats me on the back.

I can barely speak, but I manage to say, "Nothin' much, dude. How 'bout you?"

"It's chill, you know?" He turns to Katy, motions toward her, then returns his gaze to me as he says, "You know my girl, right?"

I nod and say, "Yeah, we've met." I try to give her a smile. Who the hell knows what the expression on my face actually looks like though. I say to her, "Nice to see you again."

She smiles, then shyly looks at her feet that are clad in bulky white Adidas Superstars.

Katy's cute. Short, kinda curvy. She's wearing a white tank top with super-short cutoffs that show off her smooth legs. She's nervous, I can tell. She knows Antonio. She's afraid of Antonio. Like all of us.

Carlos steps into the room from the kitchen. He and Nathan exchange a handshake-hug. My stomach twists. My neck muscles tighten. My head throbs; a pain shoots down my neck and into my jaw. The beer's not setting right either. I gotta get out of here.

Trying not to draw attention to myself, I shuffle down the hallway toward the bathroom. With the door shut, I close my eyes and rest my head in my hands. The throbbing reverberates down my arms. Beyond the door, chatter, laughter.

A hard knock on the door disrupts me. It's followed by Antonio's voice. "Hurry up."

I take a deep breath and open the door. Creepy dude is standing right there. He stares at me and then says, "C'mon, homie. We ain't got all day."

I feel my neck tighten. I say, "What about Katy?"

Dude just chuckles and says, "Don't worry about that dumb bitch. Just take care of your business."

He waits for me to leave the bathroom, then follows me to the kitchen. Carlos is sitting at the table again. Nathan is standing near him telling him some story about a car he test drove. Katy is standing next to Nathan, one hand on her hip, chomping on gum, occasionally blowing bubbles. She seems bored.

Nathan's back is to me. I can do it now. Katy though, she's close to him. I don't want to hit her on accident. Or does Antonio expect me to shoot her too?

I'm sweating more. I'm shaking. My head is pounding. I can't fucking breathe.

Nathan turns toward me and says, "Right, Mikey?"

"Wh— What?"

Nathan chuckles and says, "Jesus, bro. Don't you ever listen to shit anybody says?"

"I was in the pisser."

"Whatever, bro. I was just saying those new Corvettes are dope, right?"

I nod in agreement. It's still hard to breathe.

Nathan turns back to Carlos, and I exhale a long breath, then reach behind my back. But before I can grab the gun, Nathan turns to look at me and says, "Anyway, what ya here for, bro? You pickin' up too?"

Words won't form, so I nod in agreement.

Nathan doesn't like the look on my face though. He looks at Antonio, then to Carlos and says, "Man, what is this shit?"

Carlos stands up and Nathan seems even more nervous now. Backing away, moving toward the living room he says, "Man, fuck this shit."

Antonio blocks his path to the front door and says, "We gotta talk, homie."

Katy nervously follows her boyfriend into the living room, probably afraid to be near Antonio, but more afraid to be alone.

Nathan looks at me, then at Antonio and says, "Man, what's this shit about?"

Antonio steps closer to Nathan, says, "You been talking to the cops about me?"

"What?" Again Nathan looks at me, then at Antonio and he says, "Fuck that shit, bro. Who's been saying that?"

"Lots of people, homie. Too many."

"It's not me, bro. No fucking way. You know it ain't me."

Antonio looks at me. He nods, steps away from Nathan. He wants me to do this now. I'm shaking too much though and before I can grab the S&W from my waistband, Nathan darts toward the front door.

Antonio follows, beats him to the door, steps in his path to slow him.

I fumble for the gun.

Nathan's blocked in the entryway.

Antonio shouts, "Do it, Rojo!"

I raise the gun, train the sights on Nathan, and squeeze the trigger.

It's loud. Everything mutes for a moment. The TV. The shouting.

My ears ring, but slowly Katy's screams overpower the noise in my head.

Nathan stumbles out the front door. Katy goes after him, but Antonio blocks her path. I raise the gun again, aim at her.

She's trembling, sobbing.

I can't breathe. Air won't come in. I try to steady my hand.

Katy's breathing is choppy, irregular. Tears run down her cheek, streaking her eye makeup.

Antonio steps beside me and says, "Not her."

He takes the S&W from my hands, turns to Katy and says, "Call the cops from your cell. Say it was a drive-by. Black four-door car with big chrome rims. That's all you saw."

She sobs, shakes.

Antonio shouts, "Hey! You fucking hear me?"

She sobs louder but nods to indicate his demands have been heard.

"Get outta here then, bitch."

She stumbles through the door.

Antonio turns to me and says, "Let's go."

We walk out the door into the barren yard where Nathan has collapsed. Katy kneels beside him, balling, hyperventilating.

I can't breathe either. I can't think. My vision is blurred. The beer in my stomach bubbles, making me want to vomit.

Antonio pushes me toward the curb. Headlights—headlights approach. It's a big SUV and it stops right in front of me.

Antonio grabs a handful of my shirt, guides me toward the back seat, shoves me inside. He slides in next to me.

Carlos is in the driver seat. We pull away from the curb as Katy's screams echo across the neighborhood.

Carlos pulls up to my building and parks in front, facing the wrong direction on the street.

Antonio slides out. Carlos too.

Carlos is lighting a cigarette when I exit the SUV. The shaking has stopped, but everything feels distant, dream-like.

Antonio turns to me, pats my jaw with his meaty hand, says, "Hey, Rojo." He extends his hand to me. "Here ya go."

I place my palm under his hand. He drops it in my palm: three red balloons. Heroin, probably.

"You're back in business, amigo." Antonio smirks, then says, "Don't fuck it up again."

I nod. It's all I can do. Words refuse to exit my mouth.

Carlos takes a big drag of his cigarette, then flicks it into the street. He walks around the other side of the SUV and climbs in the passenger seat. Antonio opens the driver door and climbs in, slamming the door behind him.

The tires squeal as the SUV pulls away.

I'm alone and it's quiet, except in my head where Katy's screams still echo.

SICKO

Each pothole in the washed-out road tossed Craig in his seat and strained the suspension of his twenty-year-old truck. Flickering neon ahead guided him to the Oasis Motor Lodge, the lone building at the end of the road, located next to a puddle of river runoff just outside St. Louis, on the Illinois side of the river. Though always a fleabag motel, these days, a passerby could easily mistake it for a correctional facility—a bland two-story cinder block structure walled off by more cinder block.

The chances of finding Gavin at the Oasis weren't good. He didn't seem to go there often, but Craig had found him there once before, about a year ago, unconscious in a first-floor room with seafoam green walls and a floral-print comforter on the bed.

The Oasis wasn't the kind of place you could visit unnoticed. With just one way in and out, the manager saw every car and every person that entered the property. It didn't have a lobby—no place to enjoy a continental breakfast or to sip complementary coffee—just a window with plexiglass. Beyond the plexiglass sat a woman who'd seen far too many bad things in her numerous years of life.

She glared at him as he drove up to the window. Above her, a faded metal sign dangled from the building's crumbling facade touting queen beds, direct-dial phones, and free HBO.

He forced a smile. "Good evening. I'm looking for my nephew. His name's Gavin. He's twenty, about six foot tall—"

"I know who your nephew is. He ain't here."

"He may not be renting a room, sure, but are you positive he's not staying with someone else here?"

"I ain't seen him come or go, and I see it all."

Craig nodded, then glanced across the lot. Several of the regulars sat outside their rooms, probably seeking relief from the stifling summer humidity and the stuffiness of the cramped accommodations. "Mind if I talk to some folks? See if anyone's seen him around?"

She glared at him, shifted her gaze toward the rooms, then back to him. "Don't go pissin' no one off."

"Wouldn't dream of it."

"I mean it. One of them complains about you and I'll call the *real* cops."

An unnecessary dig. He'd told her before that he wasn't a PI. Just a concerned uncle looking for his brother's drug-addicted kid. "You've got my word." He raised his hand like he was in court. "No pissing anybody off."

She nodded her head toward the rooms. Nonverbal permission to enter the property.

He drove past the algae-plagued swimming pool and pulled his truck into a parking space in front of one of the twenty or so ground-floor rooms. Someone's belongings sat on the walkway, stacked in a pile beside a door. He climbed down from his truck, maneuvered around the mound of junk, and stepped toward the next room where a woman seated in a folding lawn chair smoked a cigarette. She wore gray sweatpants, the elastic legs pulled up to her knees, her torso covered by nothing more than a beige bra.

He nodded his chin toward her. "Evening."

She puffed, exhaled.

He stepped closer to her. "I'm looking for my nephew. Wonder if maybe you've seen him."

She stared, scanned him with her eyes, then shifted her gaze to his truck. "You some sort of sicko?"

He glanced at the word on the passenger door of the aging vehicle, spray-painted there by someone about a month ago. Despite multiple attempts to remove it, the word remained legible.

He shook his head. "I'm just an uncle looking for his nephew. Gavin's his name. About six foot tall, maybe a hundred and sixty pounds. Short hair. I've got a photo if that helps."

She stared, puffed. "Ain't seen 'im."

"Are you sure? Here, have a look." He handed her the photo.

She took it from his hand and examined it for a couple seconds, then handed it back. "Ain't seen 'im."

He thanked her, then moved onto the next room where two men stood in front of an open door. One drank from a can of Bud Light as he leaned against the doorframe.

The man eyed Craig as he approached. "You lookin' for Gavin?"

"I'm his uncle. Have you seen him?"

"Been a coupla days."

"You saw him here though?"

"Naw." The man shook his head, his greasy long hair flopped back and forth. "Saw him in town. Old North. There's a church or whatever there. They give out clothing and whatever ya need. He was there gettin' some essentials."

"Do you know what day that was?"

"Musta been Wednesday. That's when they distribute."

"Is he staying someplace around there?"

"Got no idea, brother. All I know is I seen him there. Little brick building on Thirteenth. Got a cross hangin' on the front door."

He thanked the man and moved on. Heading up the stairs he found another man sat outside a room in an inflatable chair, large black headphones over his ears. From the top of the stairway, Craig waved his arms to get the man's attention.

"Sorry to bother you, but I'm looking for my nephew."

The man grumbled as he slid the headphones from his ears to his neck. "I know who you are. Shit, dog. I know all about you. What you did, you sick fuck."

"I'm just looking for my nephew, Gavin. I have a photo."

He held the photo toward the man, but instead of taking it, he slapped his hand, and the photo floated to the ground.

The man stood from the chair. "Get yo' ass outta my face, pervert. Sick-ass fucks like you ain't welcome here."

"I just need to find my nephew."

His hand low at his side, he opened a switchblade. "What you need is to get yo' sick ass outta here before I slice you open."

"I don't mean to cause any trouble. I just want to find my nephew."

The man didn't seem open to negotiations, so Craig backed down the stairway and climbed back into his truck under the watchful eye of the woman in the bra.

He drove toward the exit where the manager awaited him.

Free from the plexiglass that protected her, she walked to his open window, shook her head. "I knew you'd go pissin' somebody off."

"My apologies. I certainly didn't mean to."

Her eyes narrowed as she studied his face. "When'd you last see your nephew?"

"It's been about six weeks since he checked in with any family. He came by my brother's place looking for some cash. He was high, so Alan sent him away. Didn't want his sister to see him in the condition he was in. Since then, no one's heard from him, and we're fearing the worst."

She nodded as though she understood the situation well. "Heroin?"

"Most likely. Possibly fentanyl too. We're not really sure though."

"Well, he'll turn up. He been missin' before, right?"

"Never like this. Not to the point where no one's seen him or heard from him. We've asked everyone who's ever been a part of his life, but none of them know anything."

"He got warrants? Might check the jails."

"No warrants—not that we're aware of. We call the jails almost every day. He hasn't been booked into any of them."

She nodded another understanding nod. "You got a number I can get you at? If I see 'em, I'll let you know."

Morning sunlight poured through the windows as Craig walked downstairs to the kitchen. His wife stood at the stove, cooking eggs in a pan. Zachary sat at the island, finishing some of last night's homework beside Savannah, who sipped orange juice as she watched cartoons.

A banging noise woke him from the dream.

His eyes opened to the familiar sights of his small townhouse. The dingy walls. The cracks in the ceiling. The old furniture he'd picked up from people on Facebook— strangers who didn't know him, didn't know the sins he'd committed. All of it made more sense than the dream.

Nothing with Laura, or the kids, had ever been close to that kind of perfection, even when the family was whole.

More banging. It came from the front door.

Shouting followed. "I know you're home. Your truck's out front."

His brother wasn't the type to just go away, so he forced himself to stand, then opened the door.

Alan didn't seek permission before stepping into the living room. "You look like shit."

"It's good to see you too."

In one hand, Alan carried a drink holder with two coffee cups. His other hand held a paper bag emblazoned with a bright orange Dunkin' logo.

He lifted the drink holder and tipped a corner of it toward him. "That one's yours. Three creams."

"Thanks."

Craig wiggled it free from the grip of the tray. Alan set the holder down on the coffee table in the living room, then plopped the bag down next to it. "I didn't know what donuts you liked, so I just got a couple glazed."

Craig glanced at the bag. "You didn't have to do that."

"Well, I heard that you were out looking for my kid, so I guess this is just me saying thanks."

"Your wife know you're here?" Diana hated him and wished Alan would cut him from their lives, more than he'd already been cut.

"Not really."

Craig nodded as he pulled the plastic lid off the coffee. The smell drifted up his nostrils and a small surge of life washed over him.

Alan freed his cup from the holder, then sat on the sofa. "Anyway, thank you. I do what I can. Search when I can, but... Well, it's a lot, and it's hard on Diana."

"Don't mention it." He sipped the coffee.

"I take it you didn't have any luck?"

Craig shook his head. "No one's seen him. Or at least they won't admit that they have."

"Where'd you check?"

"Couple of shelters. Few motels. That spot over by Busch Stadium. The flop house in Dogtown. No one I talked to was much help, and a few folks didn't like me asking around."

"I'm sure. I appreciate you asking though." Alan sipped his coffee, then set it on the table. "I wrote to a few of his friends on social media. None of 'em have gotten back to me yet though."

"What about Mackenzie? I mean, I'm sure you're trying to shield her from as much of this as possible, but has she heard from him?"

Alan shook his head. "No. But you're right, I try to leave her out of anything related to her brother."

"Like I say, hate to bring her up, but I know she's always sorta been the mediator between Gavin and you."

He nodded. "Diana calls her The Peacemaker."

"Well, anyway, sorry I wasn't more help. The only thing I can say is that it could be a good thing that no one's seen him, you know? Maybe he's not in trouble. Maybe he's just laying low."

"Here's hoping." Alan stood. "I gotta get to work. The donuts are all yours."

"Thanks." He followed his brother to the door. "I'll call you the second I hear anything."

Alan opened the door and stepped onto the porch. "Appreciate you. I know I keep saying that, but it means a lot to me that you're trying to help Gavin."

"He's like a son, you know that."

Alan nodded, stared at the front door. "Can't get that cleaned, huh?"

The word "sicko" had been scrawled in Sharpie weeks ago. He'd scrubbed and scrubbed, but the best he'd been able to do was lighten the writing a little.

Craig looked at the lettering and shook his head. "Gonna have to paint over it, probably."

"Maybe I can help with that this weekend."

"Don't worry about it. I can take care of a little painting."

"Sorry this shit keeps happening."

Craig shrugged. He was used to it. It happened the most in the weeks after his arrest. It died down for a while but increased ahead of the trial. The DA eventually dismissed the charges, which should have ended all the harassment, but instead, it caused the frequency to increase—rocks through windows, spray paint on the doors, phone calls with threatening words on the other end of the line. People eventually moved onto other things, but for the past couple years, there'd been an ebb and flow to it. Whenever Jennifer received an award or spoke at a major conference about what happened to her back in high school, Craig would get a threatening phone call or two, and occasionally a brick through a window. It'd been calm for months, but recently, Jennifer graduated from Maryville, *summa cum laude*, and she'd been awarded a prestigious internship with the governor's office. All the news coverage seemed to fuel the recent uptick in the vandalism and the threats.

Alan turned, took a step down the walkway. "Welp, I should get going."

"I'll let you know if I hear anything."

Alan nodded. "I've got several meetings today, so if you need me, just text me."

Craig watched his brother walk to the curb, watched him climb into his sensible family SUV. Craig paused before going inside, stared at the door. The faded letters mocked him: *sicko*. To his family, even Alan, that's all he'd ever be.

Mick's Bar & Grill hadn't changed a bit since Laura worked there when she was in college. So little changed at Mick's that, despite the team's move to California years ago, a Rams flag still adorned the brick wall by the pool table, pinned between a Cardinals pennant and a neon Blues sign.

Craig didn't make it to The Hill often. Too many familiar faces resided there, too many ghosts from his past.

He didn't recognize the bartender.

"What can I get you?" The bartender didn't seem to recognize Craig either, which was the most important part. If the owner—Laura's cousin—were alerted to his presence, Craig's visit would be shortened considerably.

"Busch, please."

The bartender nodded and went to work pouring the beer as Craig settled onto a wooden stool. It felt normal. Like it hadn't been at least three years since he'd sat down in Mick's. Like he was still welcomed there.

The bartender plopped a paper coaster on the bar top, then set the mug on it.

"Thank you." Craig reached in his pocket, pulled out a photo of Gavin. "You haven't seen him in here, have you?"

The man leaned across the bar, examined the photo. "Doesn't look familiar."

Craig tucked the photo away. "Thanks anyway."

"He missin'?"

"Few weeks now."

"He live 'round here?"

"No, but he's got family in the neighborhood."

"You're free to ask around. Maybe someone's seen him."

Craig thanked the bartender but stayed seated. Staring out at the old place, he could almost forget the past several years and pretend that nothing had changed—pretend that once he finished his beer, he'd go home to his family.

It wasn't *his* family anymore though. They no longer acknowledged his existence, and Laura and the kids lived with another man. A guy named Ethan, and Ethan was, apparently, everything Craig wasn't. Younger. Thinner. Richer. He had more hair and a better job too. Something in sales.

Craig had a good job once. He'd joined the police department at twenty one. He'd gotten a few promotions over the years and was close to making detective, but then, after a night at Mick's, he crashed one of the department's vehicles.

He hadn't harmed anyone in the crash and the damage was minimal. One light pole in front of a Chevy dealer on Kingshighway needed repair, and the car had some dents and scratches on a front fender. But he'd had a couple drinks before driving, and that was a bad look for the department, so he had to go. Twelve years on the force erased in that one moment.

These days, inside a house a few blocks from Mick's, down a winding road that ended in a cul-de-sac—a street lined with dozens of indistinguishable gray homes all built in the early nineties—Laura, Zachary, and Savannah lived with Ethan. Inside that house, Laura fucked Ethan, cooked his dinner, did his laundry. Zachary and Savannah called him "Dad," but none of them spoke to Craig anymore. Craig, the sicko.

Craig followed the directions from the map on his phone to the little brick home on University, arriving just as the sun began to set. He'd gotten the address from a guy they called Ori, the owner of a pawn shop in Hyde Park who often fed detectives tips about criminal activity in the area.

The house looked burned and forgotten. A mix of old and new plywood covered the windows. Dead lawn, wild weeds. According to Ori, there'd been a fire at the house several months back that forced the family out for good. Since then, squatters had taken over, and on occasion, some of them came into Ori's shop with items from the home, looking to sell them for enough to buy their next high. The house had been stripped of anything of value months ago, but Ori said that lots of addicts with nowhere else to go still crashed there.

Craig pulled a Narcan spray from his glovebox and stuffed it in his pocket, just in case he encountered someone inside the house who needed it. Around back, Craig squeezed past a broken piece of plywood and stepped inside. The smell of urine and feces assaulted him, the home long deprived of utilities and flushing toilets.

His flashlight lit a path to the living room where a man laid on a ragged sofa. He groaned at the sight of the light, likely too high to discern if anything happening around him was real or not. Garbage littered the floor—remnants of the family who once called the place home and debris from the squatters who considered the entire place a dumping ground for unwanted items.

He stepped toward the sagging staircase but stopped when a young man armed with a baseball bat appeared at the top. "Who the fuck are you?"

Craig showed his hands to prove he wasn't armed. "Name's Craig. I'm just looking for my nephew, Gavin."

The kid's posture relaxed; the bat lowered. "Who?"

"Gavin. Gavin Cole. I have a picture."

The kid walked down one step. "I know Gavin. He ain't here."

"Have you seen him recently?"

"You a cop or something?"

"Just an uncle."

The kid took a few more steps down the stairway but stopped on the landing. "Been about a week or so."

"Where'd you see him?"

"Around."

"Would you mind being more specific? I'm not going to drag him back to his parents or anything like that. We just want to know that he's okay."

The kid sized him up, stared at him skeptically, like he thought he oozed copness. "He's fine. Saw him buying cigarettes at a place near the Eads Bridge."

"Is he living around there?"

The kid shrugged. "I saw him buying cigarettes. That's all I know, bro."

"You're sure it was Gavin though?"

He nodded. "It was him. Now, get the fuck outta here." He raised the bat again.

Craig backed away. The trash beneath him crunched with each step. "Please, if you see him, just ask him to call his family. That's all we want."

The kid stared; the bat rested on his shoulder.

Craig turned and hurried toward the opening at the back. He slipped through the cracked plywood, stepped into the fresh air, and inhaled deeply.

He should have pressed the kid for more info, but the sight of the bat had frozen him in a way that surprised him.

Jennifer's brother had threatened him with a bat too, banged on his front door with it as he screamed through the window, threatening to kill him. That was how Laura learned about what happened with Jennifer, and within hours, the whole world knew. The Post-Dispatch ran the story. The TV stations had it too. His face was everywhere, and wherever he went, people deemed him a monster.

A series of bad decisions guided him into the whole mess. He'd never wanted to be a security guard, especially not at a high school. Every security guard he'd ever known had wanted to be a cop, and Craig had already been a cop. Becoming a security guard was a noticeable slide down the ladder, but it was a job.

Then he met Jennifer.

She was sixteen at the time. Cute, but in a teenager sense. She had long dark blond hair that went nearly to her waist. She loved basketball and had just secured a spot on the school's team. She got good grades. She smiled a lot. Beyond that, nothing about her seemed overly special. He wasn't attracted to her. He had no reason to be attracted to her; she was a child.

He saw her each school day, between classes, at her locker. They'd say hi as they passed each other, a common interaction he had with many of the kids at the school. Before long, they'd started chatting. About boring school things at first, but later, she shared details of her life. How her parents favored her older brother over her. How they were being too strict when it came to dating. How she didn't want to go to an aunt's house for spring break.

The aunt lived in a lakeside house in Michigan, and though Jennifer expressed excitement about spending some time on the water, she was afraid she'd be bored and didn't want to be separated from friends. He felt bad for her. As a kid, he'd spent summers in Tennessee with his father, away from his friends. Without much thought, he took a notebook from her hand and scribbled his cell number on a blank page.

She texted him about two days into spring break. They didn't talk a lot in the beginning, just a few minutes at a time, usually in the evenings as she sat alone in her aunt's house without much to do. They'd chat about what she'd done that day and about her excitement of the next school year, about the next basketball season.

When spring break ended, they continued to chat, usually at night as she readied herself for bed. After a while, she started confiding in him, telling him about boys she liked, about tests she'd failed, about things she was afraid of, like going away to college. He reciprocated, complaining about his poor health, about the pills he had to take, about the damage he'd caused to his liver from drinking too much, and about the damage he'd caused to his career by being a drunk.

As the months passed, he got more comfortable with her—so comfortable that he opened up about his marriage, told her how he and his wife hadn't been intimate for months. Told her how Laura ignored him, that he didn't think she loved him anymore.

Jennifer was caring, understanding, then she sent him a selfie. Nothing explicit. Nothing provocative. A simple picture of her dressed in a T-shirt while lying in bed, her long hair draped over a shoulder.

He typed a simple but stupid message: WISH I WAS THERE WITH U.

It was unacceptable. It was gross. It shouldn't have happened, but it did.

He never was sure if her father had been monitoring their chats for some time, or if it was dumb luck that he happened to review her messages that weekend, but either way, he read it, and within a few hours, all hell broke loose. Jennifer's brother banged on the door with a ball bat. Her father took the text message—and all of their messages—to the police. The newspaper ran the article. The TV stations showed up at his house. Laura took the kids and went to her mother's house. His former colleagues arrested him. He lost yet another job. Laura filed for divorce. And a few days after that, Jennifer's brother and two of his friends attacked him in the parking lot of a Rally's, beat him, broke his nose, cracked his ribs, then left him bleeding on the pavement beside his truck.

Around midnight, Craig headed north, armed with an address for another flop house in O'Fallon that a clerk at a smoke shop directed him to. The guy didn't know Gavin and hadn't seen him, but he said lots of people crashed at the house.

His phone buzzed as he veered toward an onramp. A number he didn't recognize.

He answered anyway. "Yeah?"

"Is this the sicko?" A woman's voice. Most harassing phone calls came from men.

"Who the fuck is this?"

"Cheryl." She coughed. "From the Oasis."

"Oh... Hey."

"Are you still looking for Gavin?"

"I am. You hear something?"

"A guy—a regular here—he was with... Well, it ain't important who he was with. Point is, I seen your nephew here about twenty minutes ago. He left with the fella. They said they's going to some club over by the river. I got directions, if ya want 'em."

He pulled to the shoulder of the road and jotted the directions down on the back of a gas receipt. After hanging up, he merged onto the highway, took the next exit, then headed east on Cass, toward the river, into an industrial part of town. The area looked like it'd been forgotten by everyone, and it was hard to imagine that any kind of business operated from the location. Vacant lots and heavily graffitied buildings lined the deteriorating roads.

His headlights illuminated the long-abandoned Cotton Belt Freight Depot at the end of the road, a bit past the railroad tracks, but before he hit the tracks, he spotted the warehouse. Cars lined the road in front and filled the vacant lot next to it.

A small group of guys stood by the door, and as he stepped out of his truck, the muffled sounds of music rumbled from inside the squat building.

One of the men nodded his chin upward as Craig approached.

Craig reciprocated. "Evening."

The man didn't speak. Neither did those standing near him.

Craig held up a photo of Gavin. "Wondered if any of you've seen this man?"

Two of the men leaned in to examine the photo. One of them nodded. "Think he's around back."

"That way?" Craig pointed toward the vacant lot on the side of the building.

The man nodded.

"Appreciate you."

It seemed Cheryl had come through for him, but as he neared the back of the building, he encountered a wall— seven feet of brick that blocked access to any other parts of the building.

Something rustled in the nearby shrubbery. He turned, shined his light toward the noise. Two men stepped out from the shrubbery—a stocky man who Craig didn't know, and Gavin. He looked worse than he ever had. Skinnier than he'd ever been.

"Gavin? It's me, Uncle Craig."

Gavin turned away from the light, shielded his eyes.

The stocky man stepped forward. "So? What ya want?"

"Gavin, I just want to know that you're all right. We're worried about you."

Gavin's gaze shifted to the ground as he rubbed his forearm with his palm.

The stocky man stepped closer. "He's fine."

"Could I speak to him alone, please?"

"Fuck off."

A group of men approached from the street, boxed him into the corner formed by the wall and the building.

"Look, I just want to know that Gavin is okay. That's all I want."

The stocky man picked up a discarded two-by-four. The men behind him closed in, cut off the possibility of escape.

Gavin slinked back, leaned against the wall. "Sorry, Uncle Craig."

Before he could respond, something hit him in the head. A blinding pain shot from his skull through his back.

As he turned to confront his attacker, the stocky guy swung the two-by-four, smashed him in the back of the head. The impact blurred his vision, sent him to one knee.

The next blow sent him to the ground where a flurry of kicks landed, bloodying his face, loosening teeth, breaking ribs.

When the assault ended, the stocky guy pushed Gavin into an SUV.

One of the men grabbed Craig's wallet and his keys. Another took his phone and watch, then delivered one more hard kick to his frail ribs. Craig heard his truck start, heard it rumble as it pulled away from the curb.

The rest of the men climbed into the SUV with Gavin and drove away, leaving Craig alone on the ground in a cloud of dust, stripped of everything left in his life.

GOOD NEIGHBORS

Later that evening, they sat together in their apartment wondering if they'd made the right decision. While they didn't know the couple next door, they'd passed them in the breezeway a few times. Once, Matt said hello to the man, but he didn't respond. Haley saw the woman near the mailboxes one afternoon, but she kept her head low, glanced at Haley through her bangs, then hurried up the stairs.

The couple moved in just weeks before the pandemic began—less than a month before the city shut down and everyone got stuck at home. The woman had a son, apparently from a different relationship. The only reason Matt and Haley knew that much was because he'd mistakenly knocked on their door a week or so after the couple moved in when he'd come to visit his mom. He seemed to be college age, but he was shy and didn't say much.

Once the lockdown began, they never saw him around. In fact, no one seemed to enter or exit the apartment next door. Food was delivered occasionally, and Haley had seen someone deliver groceries once, but the couple didn't seem to go anywhere or welcome company. They were definitely home though because Matt and Haley often heard them banging around in the kitchen. And then there was the shouting.

Neither of them thought much about it at first. The last tenants of the apartment—a father and his adult son—screamed at each other all the time, usually after a night of drinking. The apartment's walls were not thick or well insulated, so it wasn't uncommon to hear the disagreements of nearby neighbors.

This was different though. The man shouted often; the woman only cried.

"Should we call the cops?" Haley asked one night when the shouting seemed particularly violent. They'd just eaten dinner and were clearing the table.

"Maybe," Matt said while setting a plate in the dishwasher. "I'm just not sure what we'd tell them."

The disturbance subsided before they reached a decision, so they let it go and found something to watch on Netflix.

Ultimately, they felt good about not involving the police in something that seemed to be a minor argument. But just after nine the next morning, they heard more shouting, more crying.

With both of their offices still shut down, Matt and Haley were working from home, and these kinds of disturbances had become routine parts of their workday. Once again though, the shouting seemed angrier than usual.

Haley gazed at Matt over the top of her laptop monitor. "What do we do?"

"I don't know." He let out a long sigh and then said, "I feel weird calling the cops about some crying. I mean, that's not a crime, right? Crying."

"No, but something's clearly going on over there. Maybe it'd be good to have someone come out and check on the woman." Haley thought it over for a moment and then said, "But they'll know it was us that called. I'm not looking to start a feud with them."

Matt agreed and they returned to their work.

The shouting lasted about a half hour, then things were quiet the rest of the day.

It became a familiar pattern—the man shouted, the woman cried—but it never lasted long and never seemed to escalate beyond shouting and crying, at least not until that summer.

Matt and Haley were again watching TV one evening when the yelling began. This time, it was so loud it interrupted the episode of Ozark they were trying to finish.

Matt paused the show as Haley walked to the shared wall. Pressing her ear to the drywall, she heard the man grumbling just before he called the woman a "stupid bitch." Then came a thump that rattled the pictures on their walls, followed by another thud, and then a shriek from the woman.

Haley hurried back to the safety of the sofa. "Did he just hit her?"

Matt nodded. "I think so."

Haley reached toward the coffee table and grabbed her phone. "I'm calling."

Matt again nodded.

Haley dialed and began pacing the living room. The 911 operator answered quickly, and Haley relayed the name and address of the complex but stumbled to find the right words to explain why she was calling. "I'm pretty sure our neighbor just hit his wife. Or his girlfriend. I'm not sure if they're married."

The operator wanted to know if she'd witnessed it.

Haley felt stupid saying she'd only heard it—or *thought* she'd heard it, for that matter.

The operator asked if anyone's life was in danger.

Haley didn't know, of course. She'd begun to doubt what she heard, and it was impossible to know with any certainty what was happening on the other side of the wall. "I—I think so. She was crying really loudly, and the thud we heard sounded really bad."

Haley's shoulders slumped as she lowered the phone from her ear.

Matt's eyes sat wide on his face, his eyebrows high on his forehead. "What'd they say?"

"They're sending some officers."

"Good."

Haley wasn't convinced she'd done the right thing though. "Is that what's best? Cops?" She pushed a pile of magazines aside and sat down on the edge of the coffee table. "What if we're wrong about what's going on?"

"You heard that thud. That's not a normal thing."

"Are you sure the noise was part of a fight though?"

"Totally sure. Why are you suddenly doubting what we heard?"

"I don't know. I just don't want us sticking our nose into things that aren't any of our business. We've fought before. How embarrassing would it have been if the cops showed up at the door?"

"What happened was way more than an argument, babe. He clearly hit her."

"Are you sure?"

"I can't imagine what else that noise would be."

Haley stared at the ground for a moment, then nodded in agreement. "Okay. If you're sure."

It took about a half hour, but two officers showed up and knocked on the neighbors' door. Matt watched through the peephole as two men in uniforms stood in the breezeway. No one answered the door, so one of the cops knocked again. After a minute or so with no answer, both men walked away.

Haley had told the operator she didn't need to be contacted for a follow-up, so they had no way of knowing if anyone ever got in touch with the woman or not.

For two days, the couple next door made no noise at all, and Matt and Haley imagined the worst, but around dinnertime the following Friday, they heard the shouting again. An unsettling confirmation that the woman was still alive.

The couple continued to argue throughout the summer. Matt and Haley nearly got used to the yelling, but that fall, their walls shook again, followed by the woman saying, "Stop, please stop."

Matt called the cops. He gave the address, explained what they'd heard, and he too requested not to be contacted in hopes their neighbors wouldn't know who kept calling the cops on them.

It took nearly forty-five minutes for officers to show up—one male and one female—but they again left when no one answered the door. Within minutes of the officers' departure, Matt and Haley heard someone banging around in the kitchen next door.

Over the next few months, they called the cops three more times, and each time, the cops came out, knocked, and left when no one answered.

That August, when the pictures on their walls again rattled, Matt and Haley pressed their ears to the wall, hoping to hear something they could pass on to the police.

The man's words were trenchant. "You stupid whore!"

The unmistakable sound of flesh hitting flesh followed. The woman shrieked, then whimpered.

The man said, "Get up. It didn't hurt that bad."

Sobbing, the woman apologized.

Matt told the 911 operator what the man said and that the man had clearly struck the woman. It seemed to increase the urgency of the officers' response because three officers arrived within minutes.

Matt gazed through the peephole as a tall, burly male officer knocked on the door. When no one answered, he made a fist and banged harder. The sound vibrated Matt's face as he peered through the peephole.

Still, no one came to the door. Another officer stepped closer and yelled—demanding that they answer their door. "We've received multiple calls, so we know somebody's inside this apartment. We're not going anywhere until you talk to us."

It worked. The door creaked open and the man— short and overweight—stepped into the breezeway to meet the officers. Matt heard him tell them he'd been rearranging some furniture and that he couldn't imagine why people thought he was shouting. "We're just moving some stuff around the living room. That's it."

The officers asked to speak to the woman, and the man yelled over his shoulder for her. Within seconds, she appeared in the breezeway.

She spoke softly, and Matt couldn't make out what she was saying, but she seemed to corroborate the story about moving furniture.

What they'd heard was not furniture being moved, both of them were sure of that. What could they do though? They had no way to prove to the cops that he'd called her awful things, or that he'd struck her, and without evidence, their word meant nothing.

They'd planned to order from the Thai place that had just opened in the strip mall a few blocks away and then spend the evening catching up on some shows. Haley grabbed the menu from beneath the magnet on the refrigerator, then plopped down on the sofa next to Matt. She was reading him the noodle options when they heard a loud thud.

A picture vibrated off the wall and fell to the carpeted floor below. Haley gasped; Matt flinched.

The man shouted and screamed. Louder than they'd ever heard him before, like the wall wasn't there to protect them from his rage. He yelled awful things at the woman; called her terrible names. Then the familiar thud again shook the framed memories hanging on their wall.

Haley reached for her phone just as another thud rattled their world. The man released a loud groan—a pained sound that reverberated through the thin wall.

Then silence.

Matt and Haley looked at each other, then cautiously walked toward the wall and pressed their ears to it.

It was quiet on the other side, like nothing had happened, like they'd imagined the entire thing.

Leaning away from the wall, they stared at each other, afraid to make any noise—hoping to hear a sound next door, anything that indicated everyone was okay.

In a near whisper, Haley said, "What do you think happened?"

Matt shook his head and quietly said, "I'm not sure."

Haley returned her ear to the wall and Matt followed. The hum of a TV or a radio pulsated through the drywall, but it was difficult to distinguish its origins. It could have been from a neighbor downstairs, or from above them.

Matt pulled away from the wall and went toward the front door.

In a muted tone, Haley said, "Where the hell are you going?"

Matt didn't answer.

She watched as he reached the vinyl flooring of the entryway where he softened each of his steps toward the door. He leaned in and looked through the peephole.

Haley awaited an update, but when he didn't offer one, she quietly said, "Anything?"

Matt turned away from the door shaking his head. "No one's out there."

"What should we do?"

"I guess we should call the cops."

Haley stared at the floor as she twisted her wedding band back and forth. "What if..." She released a deep breath. "Do you think that was what it sounded like?"

He shrugged. "What'd it sound like to you?"

"Him dying."

Matt nodded in agreement. "We don't know what it was for sure though."

"Even if it was..." Haley twisted her ring in circles. "I—I don't want to get her in any trouble."

"What do you mean?"

"You know what I mean. If that's what happened, he..." She released another deep breath. "She was just protecting herself."

"Yeah, I guess." Matt nodded. "So? No cops then?"

Before she could respond, they heard voices next door.

Matt returned to the peephole just as the woman stepped out of the apartment pushing a carry-on-size suitcase. She paused, like she'd forgotten something, then her son exited the apartment, his white T-shirt spotted with what looked like blood.

Haley whispered, "What's going on?"

Matt waved his hand behind his back, motioning for her to be quiet. She took the hint, and Matt watched the son take the suitcase from the woman as the two walked down the breezeway, then out of Matt's sight.

Matt turned toward Haley and exhaled the air he'd been holding in his lungs. "It was the son. He and the woman just left, and I think he had blood on him."

"Are you sure?"

"It looked like blood to me. It was a white shirt with dark red splotches."

"Are you sure it wasn't some kind of screen printing?"

"The splotches weren't placed where screen printing is usually placed, and they weren't in any sort of pattern. I'm pretty sure it was blood."

She stumbled backward to the arm of the sofa and sat down. "What would we even tell the cops? I mean, can you say for sure that he was covered in blood?"

Matt shook his head. "I wouldn't say 'covered,' exactly. There were just some splotches on his shirt. I can't even say for sure it was blood. I suppose it could have been a pattern, like some kind of modern tie-dye or something."

She nodded as they stared at each other in silence. They'd reached a decision, even if neither had said it out loud.

Their apartment glowed, illuminated by flashing lights from the parking lot below. Other neighbors must have called the police, and the manager, or someone in the office, had apparently let the cops into the apartment next door.

Most of the complex's residents were either on their patios, in the breezeway, or standing in the parking lot— all of them trying to figure out what was going on, but Matt and Haley stayed put.

Then came the knock on their door.

Haley jumped, the noise a reminder of the months of turmoil next door.

Matt gazed through the peephole and let out a long sigh. Turning toward Haley, he whispered, "It's a cop."

She too spoke in a whisper. "What do we do?"

"Just stick to what we talked about, okay?"

She nodded and drew in a deep breath to steady her nerves.

Matt opened the door and peeked around it. "Yes? Can I help you?"

The officer wore no expression as he introduced himself and explained that they were investigating an incident next door, as he put it. He wanted to know if they'd heard or seen anything.

"Like what?" Matt asked.

The officer provided a short list of vague things like yelling or the sounds of a struggle.

"Nothing like that," Matt said. "Sorry."

"Were you in your residence around six thirty this evening?"

Matt nodded. "Yeah. We've been here all night."

"And you didn't hear any loud noises. Anything that seemed unusual?"

"No, sorry."

Haley stepped closer and said, "We've been watching TV in the bedroom. We only came out because we saw all the flashing lights."

The officer glanced at the notebook in his hand.

Haley attempted to sound calm as she said, "Is um... Is everything okay?"

The officer's face remained expressionless. "I'm afraid a man was stabbed in a nearby apartment. We don't believe any other residents are in danger, but the man did succumb to his injuries."

"That's awful," Haley said.

The officer nodded. "So, if you think of anything that you saw or heard, would you please give me a call." He handed Matt a business card.

Matt took it from him, slid it into his pocket without looking at it. "We will. For sure."

The officer left and Haley collapsed onto the couch the moment the door closed. "He knew we were lying."

"He didn't know anything."

"We just helped someone get away with killing another person. I know that woman is finally safe now, but... Should we have told them what we know? Wouldn't that help her more?"

"Maybe. Or maybe they'd never consider any of what we heard in the past and just call this a murder."

The word hung in the air between them. *Murder*. Until now, Haley hadn't thought of it that way. She stared at her bare feet. "Where do you think she is?"

"The woman?"

Haley nodded.

"I don't know." Matt shrugged. "Her son seemed to have a plan. He probably got her out of town. Maybe even out of the country. Wherever she is, it's better for her now."

"I hope so."

Matt sat down beside Haley, rested his hand on her leg. Setting her hand on top of his, she interlaced their fingers and stared toward the apartment next door, the wall illuminated by alternating red and blue light that pulsated at increasingly predictable intervals. It was oddly beautiful in a way. A mottled reminder of the decision they'd made.

QUALITY TIME

The dead guy was a problem. We could easily ditch the other things, like the bloody rug or the gun used to shoot the dude, but since his massive whale-like body was spread across the living room floor, we'd have to deal with that first.

I had no idea what to do with him. Dude had to weigh more than 300 pounds, and aside from the struggles of moving such a large piece of meat, there was also the issue of where to move it to.

Not long after the fat dude stopped twitching, my grandpa went to the garage and left me with the body—left me to freak out and to imagine what life in prison would be like. But before my imagination ran too wild, he returned with some work gloves and a box of lawn and leaf bags.

He wrapped one of the huge bags over the dude's head and half his torso, then tossed me a pair of gloves. After I slid them on my hands, he tossed me the roll of bags and said, "Wrap his legs."

I did what I was told, but as I began stuffing the fat dude's legs into a bag, Grandpa got up and left the room again. I slid the bag over the legs, but even with one bag over the top portion of the body and another over the lower portion, we were left with a good two feet of the dude's huge belly showing.

I stood up and examined the dead guy and my mind again flashed to a prison cell. Bunk beds. A stainless steel toilet. A cellmate named Bubba or some shit who couldn't wait to pound me in the ass.

The horrible image was mercilessly shattered by the sound of Grandpa's voice. "Hey, J.J."

I looked up to see a roll of duct tape flying toward me. I reached for it, bobbled it between my hands a couple times, then gained control of it.

He knelt by the corpse, tucked some of the trash bag tighter around the torso, and said, "Tape it in place."

Fumbling with the roll of tape, I spun it in my gloved hands as I searched for the frayed end. I pulled about a foot of tape away from the roll before I knelt beside Grandpa and secured the bag to the fat dude's body. I had no idea what was next. No fucking clue what we were gonna do with the massive body. I didn't even know who the dude was or why he showed up at the house. No idea how in the hell my grandpa, at nearly eighty, beat the shit out of the dude before shooting him.

It all happened fast. It was like four in the afternoon, and we'd just gotten back from a doctor's appointment. See, for nearly a year now, I've been driving Grandpa around, helping him into a wheelchair and into medical offices for a slew of appointments—everything from routine checkups to physical therapy for his messed-up leg.

My sister accused me of trying to get into the old man's will, but that's not it. I just wanted to help; just wanted to spend some time with the man and get to know him. And honestly, I don't think my grandpa has much to leave behind anyway. Sure, his house is hella nice, but the garage is filled with a busted down eighties Ford pickup and a late-nineties Lincoln Town Car, a sedan that was top of the line back when I was born. He also watches TV on an old twenty-five-inch tube television, top of the line around the time the Town Car still turned heads. The ancient thing needs a converter box to receive today's digital signals, and the remote is held together with electrical tape.

Anyway, my sister is cracked. I'm just trying to do the right thing for an old man who shares some of my DNA. He needed help with some basic things, and so when my ma suggested that I move out to Vegas to assist him in his day-to-day life, I figured, why the hell not? Vegas sounded cool. A twenty-four-hour town filled with cash, sexy bitches, and more sunshine in one day than I'd seen in six months in Cleveland. Ma also offered to help with my relocation costs, so it'd have been stupid as hell for me to turn all that shit down.

So, that's what I've been doing for the past several months. Helping out with a trip to *this* doctor, a trip to *that* doctor. Occasionally we stopped for a bite to eat at a pizza joint. On a really special day, maybe even the Cracker Barrel.

I didn't have much keeping me in Cleveland, so I loaded my car with the few decent belongings I owned, filled up the tank, and made the two-thousand-mile drive. I had a place to live lined up before I hit the road—a nice one-bedroom apartment just off the Strip, or so I thought. I mean, the place is nice enough, that part's for sure, but I soon came to learn that just because a place is on Las Vegas Boulevard doesn't mean it's on the Strip. See, my place is south of all the cool stuff. South of the airport even, like *way* south—a good five miles from the closest Strip resort. But hey, it is near the Cracker Barrel, so I've got that going for me.

Anyway, today started out like most days with Grandpa. Our trip to the doctor was basically like all the others. I picked my grandpa up at his place out in Summerlin—dude lives in a fancy neighborhood and has a massive house with a pool, tons of palm trees, and a sweet-ass view of the city. The place has four bedrooms and nearly four thousand square feet, but my grandpa lives alone. Not sure why I don't use one of the bedrooms instead of paying rent for my lame-ass little apartment, but he's never offered, and I've never asked.

Fuck, I'm rambling. My point is, I schlepped my ass all the way out to Summerlin and helped him get from the house to the passenger seat of my Nissan, buckled him in, then drove him to his doctor's office out by the hospital. I parked my car, hopped out, grabbed a wheelchair from the lobby, helped him into it, and wheeled him into the waiting room, just like always.

I'd planned to chill there with him until the staff took him to an exam room for his two o'clock appointment, but the old man insisted I should leave. Said he'd call me when he was done. Fine. I never hang out where I'm not wanted, so I stepped outside, sat on the little stucco wall by the wheelchair ramp, and stared at my phone for a while. You know, a little Instagram, a little YouTube. Just some mindless bullshit to kill the time. Nothing seemed weird about anything around me. I mean, yeah, looking back, sure, I remember seeing some shit that's odd, but at the time, nothing sounded any alarm bells. But as I said, looking back, I can remember seeing the same car drive by a couple times: a black Challenger SRT. Thing was fucking sweet. Super dark window tint, black rims, red brake calipers. It drove by a few times, went real slow, circled the lot. I thought nothing of it though. Just assumed they were looking for an address or trying to see if a specific doctor's name was on the sign out front.

What's that old saying about hindsight? It's twenty-twenty or whatever? So yeah, in hindsight, I remember seeing the dead dude there too. I mean, he was alive then—walked right by me while I sat outside the place. Tall, bald, fat as fuck. I totally remember him now. Dude was looking at me a little weird, and at first, I thought he looked familiar, like a dude I met during my five-month stay at the Cuyahoga County Corrections Center a couple years back. I checked the dude out as he walked by, but after a bit, I realized it wasn't the same guy. For one, he was older than the dude I was thinking of, and second, it was unlikely that the same dude I met in lockup out in Cleveland was here in Vegas now too.

Anyway, the guy glared at me a bit, then moved on. That was right before the black Challenger drove by for the third time. It moved quicker that time, and as it turned out of the medical complex toward Charleston Boulevard, the tires squeaked a little. So what, right? That shit goes on all the time. Don't mean nothin', at least I thought it didn't mean nothin'. And nothin' happened then anyway. The Challenger accelerated onto Charleston, and soon after, Grandpa called and said he was finished at his appointment. So I pulled my car up to the front door, helped him back into it, and then we grabbed a bite to eat at this little Italian joint on the outskirts of downtown. Just another day.

Shit got weird when we got back to Grandpa's house though. See, normally, I pull up in front, help him into a wheelchair, then roll him inside, get him comfortable. Once he's in his house, he doesn't use the chair to get around. Fucking place has an elevator, so he doesn't even have to worry about going up any stairs. So, I usually get him to the couch, flip on his old-ass TV, and dip. Sometimes I go back to my tiny apartment, sometimes I hit up a sportsbook to watch a game. Otherwise, I just go home, have a beer or smoke a preroll and relax. I don't know many people out here, so I rarely do anything else.

Anyway, I never got around to deciding what to do after dropping Grandpa off because before I even pulled into the driveway, he told me to stop.

"Cut the engine," he said as he rolled down the passenger window.

"What? Why?"

"Just do it."

I did it.

He stuck his head out the window and stared toward the end of the block.

I waited for further instruction. None came, so I said, "What are we doing?"

"Wait here," he said before opening the door and getting out of my car.

Grandpa walked all the way up the driveway, then crouched behind some shrubs, all without the help of a wheelchair or even a walker.

Once I lost sight of him, I sat quietly in my car, but that felt wrong. What if he fell? What if his messed-up leg failed him? I couldn't wait, so I got out of the car and followed the path he'd taken toward the house.

I was about halfway up the driveway when I heard a car accelerate and tires squeak. I glanced down the street toward the noise and spotted the black Challenger with the red calipers turning onto the main road before disappearing from sight. I didn't have much time to think about it because my attention shifted to the house where I heard grunts and shouting. I jogged toward the noises and that's when I found grandpa hitting the fat fuck in the face with the butt of a revolver a buncha times. The mass of blubber stumbled backward toward the living room, and that's when Grandpa pointed the pistol at him and fired three or four rounds.

Before I could process any of what happened, Grandpa tossed me the roll of garbage bags and I found myself wrapping the fat fuck in plastic. But as I secured the bags with the duct tape, all kinds of shit came to mind—mostly things I'd heard about my grandpa throughout my life. Shit about how he was a made member of the Cleveland crime family. How he'd moved out to Vegas in the late seventies, supposedly to oversee the family's interest in rackets out here. I never really believed any of that shit. Sure, he was known as "Johnny Vegas," and growing up, people always talked shit about him, saying things like, "He's a mob boss," or "He's a killer," or whatever, but I didn't necessarily believe it. Now, I admit, I used it to my advantage. Like, when I first started high school, a few weeks in, a couple of pricks started some shit with me. I got in their faces and said something like, "Do you know who I am? I'm John Mancuso's grandson. All I have to do is tell him your name and someone will be dragging your dead body out of Lake Erie."

Now, at that time, I didn't really believe Grandpa was in the mob, but even if he was, I knew he wasn't going to have a couple of punk-ass bitch high schoolers whacked on my order, but that shit worked. Both of those shitheads backed off and left me alone the rest of high school, probably because rumors spread across school that my grandpa had a kid killed a year before I started at that school because he'd gotten handsy on a date with my sister. I'd always heard the kid drowned while kayaking, and hell, that's probably what happened, but a bunch of people at my school were convinced that Grandpa had the guy killed and that his mob associates dumped the body in a lake.

Anyway, before long, most everyone at my high school was afraid of me. I didn't think too much about it at the time, I mean, throughout elementary and middle school, me and the other Italian kids had a bunch of shit talked about us, like people always accused our family members of being in the mob. It was stupid high school shit, right? I mean, I talked shit about the Irish kids all the time, called their parents drunks, said all they did was get into fights. Sure, it probably wasn't true, but that's what we did. We were dumbass kids. I didn't mean most of the shit I said back then, and that's why I never took the shit that was said about my family very seriously. So when some kids at school started saying that my dad had been a mafia capo and that he'd been killed because of it, I didn't pay much attention. I mean, I didn't know my dad well. He died when I was eight—some kind of on-the-job accident. He was a truck driver and had a crash on a highway outside of Youngstown. He often delivered shit to construction sites, and I'd always heard there was some kind of accident where some shit wasn't secured properly and shifted during transport, caused his truck to jackknife.

I was young as shit, so I don't remember much about those days. I remember some union rep coming to our house one night to ensure my mom the union would take care of the family. I don't remember much else. I was eight. Just a kid. I didn't understand much of it either, and I went on without a father. Some uncles stepped in. They took me to Browns games, Indians games. Took me fishing. Taught me to shoot a gun. All the shit Dad would have done, if he'd lived. Eventually, I moved on with life. Made some friends, limped through school, and managed to graduate. I got a job. I got into some shit. Got thrown in jail. Got out. Got into some more shit. Went back to jail. You know, life stuff.

After my first stint inside, I got a job literally flipping burgers at a shitty fast-food restaurant. It was fine. It paid my rent, and they were willing to hire me in spite of my record. But there, I met this dude who said his dad had known my dad. Said all that shit about my dad being a truck driver was total bullshit. Said my dad didn't die in a crash but instead was killed by some dude named Frankie Prata. Said that Frankie Prata shot my dad to death in the back hallway of some dive bar in Glenville.

This was all news to me, so I hopped on Google and started digging around a little. Looked up this Prata motherfucker. Yup, sure as shit, apparently he ran some crew in Detroit for years before eventually becoming underboss of the Detroit Partnership. And apparently he played a big role in taking out a bunch of mobsters in Cleveland, which weakened the organization to the point of near collapse.

So then I searched for news stories about my dad. I typed "Joey Abruzzo" into the search bar.

Nothing.

He and I share the same name, and I found more about myself than I did him. Everyone called him "Joey A," and so they started calling me "Joey Junior," then "Joey J." I fucking hated it because I felt like it put me in the shadow of a man I didn't even know. I tried to get people to call me Joseph, but settled on being called J.J.

Anyway, online, it was like my dad never existed. Nothing about him dying in a crash near Youngstown. Nothing about him being a truck driver. Nearly out of ideas, I searched for "Joey A" along with Prata's name, and that's when I found my dad's name mentioned on a website about the mafia—one brief mention that credited Frankie Prata with killing my pops. Shit didn't come with any evidence though. Coulda been based on the same hearsay that the pricks at work spouted off with.

Goddamnit. I keep trailing off. Bunch of my teachers thought I might have that ADHD shit. Maybe so. Anyway, back to the fat dead guy that grandpa shot. We got his bulbous stomach wrapped, and then we moved onto securing trash bags all the way around his body. I had to shove my shoulder into his back and push with all my weight to get him rolled over so we could wrap his back. I stretched a trash bag out across his massive frame, and Grandpa stepped in with the tape.

Grandpa held the roll away from his chest, stretched the last of it out, stuck it in place on the fat guy, and gave it a hard slap.

We were done wrapping him up, but that's when it hit me: we'd have to get rid of the plastic-wrapped clump of meat somehow.

Grandpa tossed the empty roll of tape into the kitchen garbage. "That's all the tape I've got, so it'll have to do." He opened the door that led to the garage. "I got shovels out here."

That's when another thing hit me: Grandpa wanted *me* to deal with the dead guy. I didn't say anything. Just stared at the sack on the floor—the fat motherfucker covered head to toe in plastic and silver tape.

"You can use my car. The trunk is bigger than that little sports car you drive." Grandpa tapped me on the shoulder. I turned, faced him. He smashed the keys into my palm.

I stared at them, then nodded in agreement, like it was no big deal—like I loaded dead guys into trunks at least once a week. One question came to mind though, so I asked it. "Where the fuck do I take him?"

"Deep in the desert is best, but the ground is going to be damned hard this time of year, and, well..." He stared at the fat fuck on the floor. "This coglione will require a big hole." Grandpa peered into the garage again. "Okay, new plan. Lake Mead is a good option. Lake Mohave or Lake Havasu, if you're up for the drive." He pointed to a corner of the garage. "I got a few cinder blocks stacked up back there. Got some rope over there too. Make sure you tie the blocks to the body real good so it don't come floating back up."

Again I nodded, not because any of this was familiar to me, but because at least it answered the question of what I was supposed to do with the dead dude.

Grandpa patted me on the back. "You did come all the way out to Vegas to help, didn't you? To become part of the family, right?"

I nodded. "Yeah."

"Well, you wanna earn your button, don't ya? This is a good start."

"Can I ask one question?"

"Shoot."

"Who is he?"

He points at the mound of plastic. "This fuck? I think his name's Gabriel. Not sure, but I know he's out of Detroit."

"Yeah? Why was he in your house?"

"Jesus, don't you know any of what's going on? I figured your mom woulda told you a few things about her old man. I figured that's why she sent you out here."

He stared at me.

I didn't know what he was talking about. "She... I—I haven't heard anything."

"Okay, it's like this: there's been a few shake ups lately. Buncha guys out in Chicago got picked up on federal charges. With them going away, things are a bit... fragile. The Cleveland family's been hanging on by a thread, and Chicago, well, the Outfit's been keeping us going, but with those guys going away, those fucks in Detroit have been moving on us, looking to take all of us out. That's what Shamu here came to do. Take me out."

"So... If you hadn't killed him, he'd have killed you?"

"You fuckin' bet he would have. C'mon, kid. Surely you know all this shit. You know what happened to your dad, don't you?"

"The trucking accident?"

"Jesus... Is that really what you think happened? You probably still think that black lab you got when you were twelve moved to a farm too." He shook his head and stared at his loafers. "I guess we need to have a talk. C'mon, I'll ride with ya. We'll get rid of the whale, and then I'll tell you about your pops."

With the sun setting, Grandpa directed me way out of town—far south near the end of Rainbow Boulevard and out onto some unpaved roads. The rear end of the Town Car scraped the ground with every dip in the washed-out roadway.

I stopped when the road ended, blocked by fencing from some sort of storage yard. "Want me to turn around?"

"Not until we get rid of the cargo in the trunk." He opened the passenger door and stepped out of the car.

I got out too, looked around. "There's no water out here. What's the plan."

Grandpa pointed toward a parked train. "Shamu's gonna ride the rails."

I looked at the train, a mix of closed-up box cars and centerbeam cars loaded with lumber and other building materials. "Are you serious? Won't someone find him?"

Grandpa took the keys from me and headed toward the trunk. "So what? He's out of my house." Grandpa lifted the trunk lid then gazed toward one of the trains as he slid work gloves onto his hands. "Let's hope this thing's headed to Detroit. It'd be nice of us to send this fuck home, don't ya think?"

I gloved my hands and then pulled on the mass of wrapped human. Together, Grandpa and I lifted him over the edge of the trunk and let his stiffening body slam to the ground beneath us, basically the reverse of how we'd gotten him in the trunk to begin with. From there, we dragged his fat ass over to the awaiting train, and once again hoisted him off the ground, swung him a little, then heaved him onto an empty centerbeam car.

Grandpa lost his footing and leaned into the railcar for support.

I reached to grab him. "Are you okay?"

"I'm fine. I'm fine." He struggled to take breaths. "Just way to fucking old to still be doing this shit."

I leaned against the railcar, looked around the industrial area, then at my able-bodied grandfather. "So, I have to ask. Your leg. The wheelchair. All of that is bullshit?"

He chuckled. "The leg's fine. I'm fine. The frail old man thing is a ruse. It keeps the feds, and our enemies, thinking I'm retired. That I'm done for. Plus, the fake health problems make a great cover for me while I'm taking care of our business out here."

"What business is that?"

"Fake scripts. Ozempic's a hot seller right now. This bit with the bum leg gives me a good excuse to do business inside exam rooms where the feds aren't likely to have bugs planted. It also gives me a good reason to meet with clinic managers in a setting that doesn't conjure too many questions from onlookers."

"So, that's what I've been helping you with?"

"Yeah. I thought you knew that."

I shook my head. "I had no idea."

"Jesus... my daughter. I figured she'd have said something to you, but I should know. She's never liked the things I do to put food on our table." He removed a glove from his left hand, then the right. "I figured you were out here because you wanted to wet your beak. Or maybe because you wanted to take out the guy who killed your old man."

"You know who killed him?"

"Do you think you're ready for that truth?"

I nodded.

Grandpa pointed at the Town Car. "Let's get outta here first."

Out of instinct, I opened the car door for him, but he was clearly capable of getting around on his own. I hopped in, started the car, turned around, headed back to the main road.

Grandpa stared forward without saying a word, so I asked the question that was on my mind. "What happened to my dad?"

"It's a bit of a long story."

"I've got the time."

He nodded. "Well, your old man worked for Carlo Sala for years. Sala was a capo in the Chicago Outfit. Your dad was up and coming—a good earner—so at some point, Sala sent him out to Cleveland. He led a crew out there for years, and from what I know, they earned big. Sala answered to a guy named Frankie Prata though, and Prata thought your dad was skimming. He thought that he wasn't kicking up what should be kicked up."

"Prata was with the Outfit?"

"He was with the Detroit guys. Back then though, they worked closely with Cleveland and Chicago. Everybody had an understanding in those days. Guys worked all over, with the blessing of bosses in each territory. All of it was routine, but once Prata got it in his head that your dad was screwin' him, he summoned your dad to a meeting at this little bar the Pratas owned. Sala was supposed to be there too, so your dad felt safe about it all, but apparently Prata didn't actually tell Sala about it. The whole thing was a setup. An ambush."

"Prata killed my dad?"

Grandpa nodded. "Your dad showed up, stood his ground, swore to Prata that he wasn't skimmin' nothing, but Prata shot him dead, right there in the bar."

"Why the fuck has everyone lied to me about the truck crash then?"

"The lie became the truth, you know? The thing about the crash, that was the official story. Prata and his crew had a buncha Youngstown cops on the payroll, so they had 'em write up reports about the supposed crash. And your mom, well, for a long time, she didn't even know what happened. By having your dad's death classified as work related, the union and the trucking company took care of you and your sister—kept your mom from having to work, you know? I'm sure she found out the truth at some point, and I know she never really bought the truck crash story, but it was just easier for everyone if that lie became true."

I loosened my grip on the wheel when my hands began to throb. I hadn't realized I'd been gripping it so hard, but I was pissed. I'd been fed total bullshit my whole life. For nearly thirty years, I'd had no idea who my father really was. But then one particular question rose to the top, so I asked Grandpa: "Is Prata still alive?"

Grandpa nodded. "Retired, but alive, yes. He's been out here for decades, bettin' on games and soaking up the sun."

"He's in Vegas?"

He nodded. "Lives out by Lake Las Vegas. He's got himself one of those McMansion townhouses on a golf course with mountain views from the hot tub. I hear he's not big on technology or security. Doesn't have cameras, doesn't employ bodyguards. It'd be really easy for someone to get to him. Easy for someone to kill him."

I turned my head and looked at Grandpa. "You want me to kill him?"

Grandpa shook his head. "If he dies, it's all-out war with Detroit. Anyone who kills him would be kicking the shit outta one big hornets' nest."

My eyes back on the road, I thought things over. Grandpa's message was mixed. War sounded bad, but why else would he have told me that the man who killed my father lived minutes away. Why else would he have told me that the man has no security protecting him, or that if I were to kill him, the likelihood of being caught was low?

Anyway, as I thought about all that stuff, Grandpa reached into the glove box and pulled out a semi-automatic pistol. He set it in his lap and dug around the glove box some more, then pulled out a suppressor. Threading it onto the barrel of the gun, he said, "Of course, hornets are pests, and any pest should be eliminated."

As we wound around the lake on the nicely paved roads, I pictured what was next. I envisioned doing it just as Grandpa suggested: Ring the doorbell, wait for the door to open, raise the gun, pull the trigger, keep pulling it until I'm sure the guy is dead.

Grandpa was quiet as we drove into the neighborhood, I assumed his silence was to let me wrap my head around everything. Everything that had happened to my family. Everything I had to do to make that shit right.

He texted someone, set the phone down, and pointed ahead of us. "Next right, up there after the roundabout.

I followed his directions but panicked when I saw the little guard shack at the front of the neighborhood. Of course a retired mob boss would live in a gated community. Why wouldn't he? We'd have to regroup. Figure out a plan to kill him somewhere other than his home.

"Turn here," Grandpa said as he pointed toward the guard shack.

"What about the..." Before I finished the sentence, I noticed the shack was empty and the gate was wide open.

Grandpa picked up his phone and waved it in the air. "I let them know it was break time."

Down the street, along one of the fairways, sat a cluster of buildings with Spanish tile roofs. Grandpa pointed and said, "That one, on the end. That's it."

He held the pistol by the barrel, offered it to me.

I took a deep breath and accepted the gun.

He nodded. "You can do this. It's in your blood."

Stepping out of the Town Car, I kept the gun at my side, walked to the door. I pictured my pops there with me. Standing to the side, ready to witness everything that was to come. Ready to get revenge on the man who took him from his family, who robbed his children of having their father be in their lives.

With my free hand, I pushed the doorbell. A chime played a pretentious melody. Then the door swung open. Behind it, an old man with a cane, age spots covering his face and bald head. I felt bad for him, until the image filled my mind, one of him raising a gun, pointing it at my father, killing the man I never got the chance to know.

"Frank?" I said.

The man nodded. "Yes? Can I help you?"

"Frankie Prata?"

"Yes. Do I know you?"

"I'm Joey J, Joey Abruzzo's kid."

I didn't await a response, just raised the gun and did what I'd come to do. And that was it. That's how Frankie Prata met his demise, and that's how I became the future of the Cleveland family.

BANKRUPT

Preston stepped into the hotel's eleventh-floor ballroom and stared at Lake Michigan through the floor-to-ceiling windows. It was a nice view, but it was also a waste since it would be pitch black outside by the time the gala began.

Shifting his gaze from the windows, he scanned the crowded room from the doorway until he located his company's three tables on the other side of the immense room, right next to the soon-to-be viewless windows. The simple banquet tables—draped lazily in white tablecloths—were costing him ten grand apiece, and he wasn't entirely sure what the money went to either. The foundation hosting the gala had something to do with funding entrepreneurship programs in Chicago high schools, or some bullshit like that.

The agreement to buy the tables had been signed by his father years ago, back when he ran Carter & Nichols. The company's lawyers said it was possible to back out of the multi-year agreement, but the PR folks were concerned about the optics of such a move. So, thirty grand later, Preston entered the ballroom ready to exchange pleasantries with people he didn't know.

He'd taken all of five steps into the room before someone called for him. "Mr. Nichols? Excuse me."

Preston released a sharp sigh, then turned toward the voice. "Yeah?"

An aging portly man stood before him, his poorly fitted department store suit a dead giveaway that he was a nobody who'd dropped $350 on a ticket to the gala in hopes of rubbing elbows with his business heroes.

"Sorry to bother you, but I'm Duane Douglas, CEO of Vanuvia Systems."

No bells were rung by any of those words. Preston offered his hand. "Nice to meet you."

"You as well! It's such an honor, sir." His face aglow with excitement, the man eagerly shook his hand. "I was just reading about your bankruptcy acquisition of Cerova Corp." His eyes widened. "Three million? From what I know about their technology, I'd say you got yourself one heck of a deal."

"Yes, well, we were certainly pleased."

"What do you plan to do with the company? If you don't mind my asking?"

"Nothing's been decided yet. And the judge still has to sign off on the deal, so for now we're not counting any chickens, if you know what I mean."

"Sure. Yeah, that makes sense. Well, I just wanted to say congrats on that deal." He reached into his pocket and pulled out a business card. "And hey, I was thinking, if you have some time, maybe I could tell you a little about my company."

Preston gazed toward his company's tables, hoping to get the attention of his VP of finance so he could bail him out of the tedious interaction. Unfortunately, Wes was seated facing the windows, his back to the ballroom.

Preston decided to use Wes as an excuse anyway. "I'm afraid I have someone waiting for me." He motioned toward the handful of people seated at the tables.

The man held the business card toward him. "No problem. Maybe I could send you a business plan that lays out our goals and details our capital needs. We've got some big plans, but we'll need funding to get to the next level."

Preston smiled politely. *Jesus. This guy must watch a lot of Shark Tank*. "Venture capital isn't exactly what we do at Carter & Nichols."

"Oh, um, I—I know, but I was hoping to partner with one of your many companies. I really think that with the right partner, and with your insight, Vanuvia would really soar."

"Okay." Preston took the card from his hand. "I'll have my guys take a look. It was nice to meet you, Doug."

"Uh, it's Duane. Duane Douglas."

Preston feigned a smile and shook the man's hand one more time. "My apologies. Enjoy your evening, Duane."

Guys like Duane were what made these events so annoying. At the same time, guys like Duane also made it worth his time to attend. He was the kind of guy who would hand over every valuable part of his company—on a silver platter—as long as he thought he was a part of something big. But Duane had no place in the tech world. The signs were so obvious they may as well have been advertised with flashing neon.

For one, Duane was too old, which probably meant that the guy's kids were the programmers in the operation while their dad—probably a former middle manager who was recently laid off—stepped in to run the company. Something to do to make him feel useful and needed until he was able to find steady work. Or until the company his kids started took off and secured his retirement. Whichever came first.

Duane was a lamb on its way to the slaughter. Chances were that his kids were working on some new app, and chances were that Carter & Nichols already owned a company (that owned a company that owned a company) with a patent for a similar technology. In a few weeks, Duane would be reading a cease and desist letter from said company—a company buried so deep in the corporate structure that he'd have no idea that Carter & Nichols was involved at all. At that point, Duane and his kids would face the tough decision to either pay a hefty fee to license the tech behind their app or shut down their business altogether.

Preston joined Wes at the table. The new kid, Cameron, was sitting next to him. A fresh Dartmouth grad who'd not yet proven himself worthy of the opportunity granted to him.

Preston tossed the business card on the ten-thousand-dollar table, then collapsed into a chair.

Wes eyed it. "What's that?"

"More hopes and dreams of jerk-off wannabe tech entrepreneurs." He slid the card toward Wes. "Have your team dig into this company. See if they've got anything we want."

Wes nodded his chin at the table to the left. "Speaking of things we might want."

Preston glanced toward the table where two girls sat with a group of people gathered around them. "Who are they?"

"Tonight's guests of honor. Emily Greener and Miranda Hayward."

"Am I supposed to know who the fuck they are or what they do?"

Wes shrugged. "They built an app together when they were in high school, and it gained some good popularity. It's one of those brightly colored games with cute animals that's supposed to teach the importance of being nice and building friendships."

"I think I just threw up in my mouth."

"Right?" Wes smirked. "But that was then. Now they're both graduates of Northwestern's Kellogg business school, and for the past couple years they've been working on some new software that uses AI technologies and data mining to analyze human behavior to predict interests."

"Yeah? What's the practical use for that?"

"It's got a ton of commercial appeal. For instance, it'll figure out what kind of music someone might be interested in, or what clothing they might want to purchase. Some major online retailers have already offered to buy their company, but they've turned down every offer."

"Is that so? What's their company's name?"

"Blossom Ridge Technologies."

"Sounds like a company run by the Powerpuff Girls."

Wes snort-laughed. "They named it after the street they grew up on together out in Bolingbrook. Adorable, isn't it?"

"Let me guess: they started the company in their garage, just like Jobs and Wozniak?"

"Something like that. Emily is the one with the brown hair. She's the company's CEO. Runs the day-to-day stuff. Miranda's the one with the purple hair. She's their chief technology officer. Oversees development, manages programmers. Shit like that."

"Their software relies on AI?"

"Largely, yeah."

Preston smiled. Carter & Nichols had been investing heavily in companies with AI patents, and chances were good that the girls' software operated on technologies similar to patents already owned by Carter & Nichols. Or at least close enough that their lawyers could threaten the Blossom Ridge girls into paying licensing fees to avoid being sued out of existence.

Preston stood, brushed off his jacket, adjusted the knot of his tie.

Wes eyed him suspiciously. "Where are you going?"

"To introduce myself. I mean, they are the guests of honor after all. It'd be rude of me not to say hi."

Wes pointed at him. "Dressed like a wolf? Why? Is your sheep costume at the cleaners?"

The crowd around the table was large, mostly bright-eyed twenty-something girls that fell into one of two categories: those eager to get a selfie with the creators of a sickeningly cute game they'd grown up playing, or those who kept babbling about glass ceilings and girls kicking ass in a male-dominated industry.

Emily looked good, wearing a green one-shoulder gown that hugged her body tightly. It looked natural on her, like she enjoyed life's finer things. Miranda, conversely, looked uncomfortable in her strapless black gown. Her bright, half-sleeve tattooed right arm also stood out in a room filled with more conservative patrons.

Once the last of the giggling fangirls stepped away, Preston approached the duo and offered his hand to each.

"Ms. Greener, Ms. Hayward. Preston Nichols the Third. It's so nice to meet you both."

Miranda smiled. "Thank you."

Preston pulled out a chair next to Emily and sat down. It was best to seem casual while hunting; it helped calm the prey. "I've heard some great things about your company. And AI, that certainly is an exciting industry, isn't it?"

Emily's eyes narrowed as she studied his face. "It is. I think we've only begun to scratch the surface of what's capable."

"Oh, for sure." Preston nodded eagerly, pretending to give a shit about the girl's sanctimonious TED Talk. "I was hoping to learn a little bit more about the AI behind your latest work. Is it something you built from scratch? Or are you currently licensing existing technologies?"

The two girls looked at each other like each wanted the other to answer the question.

Before any answer came, Miranda grabbed the purple clutch sitting on the table in front of her, then stood. "I'm sorry." She glanced at Emily. "We're supposed to do a photo op with some donors. There'll be a whole presentation later about our software. I think it'll answer all your questions."

Emily stood. "Oh, right. The photo shoot. I'd forgotten. Please excuse us."

Before Preston could respond, both girls hurried away, Emily's ass hugged by the fabric of her gown. She didn't seem to be wearing underwear, and that made him want to follow her out of the room.

The moment was interrupted by a chuckle from Wes.

Preston rejoined him at the table. "Something funny about that?"

"Sorry. I was laughing at how afraid of you they are."

"Yes, well, it seems my reputation precedes me. It doesn't matter. I'll still get the info I need, but I may have to approach things differently."

Cameron raised his hand slightly, his pointer finger aimed at the ceiling, like he was in middle school wanting to ask the teacher for a hall pass.

Preston stared at him. "Yes, you in the back. Did you have a question?"

His face reddened. "I... Um, I—I might be able to help. I know Emily Greener. We went to the same church growing up, and I helped her with a presentation for a pitch competition in Minneapolis a few years ago."

Preston smiled. The kid was a doofus, but he might prove to be a useful doofus.

He stood, changed chairs, sat beside Cameron. "I knew I liked you, Cam." He draped his arm across Cameron's shoulders. "You good with me calling you Cam?"

"Uh... Yeah. Sure."

"Cam, we're going to go downstairs to the hotel bar and I'm going to buy you the most expensive glass of single malt scotch that your guileless lips have ever touched. And I'll keep them coming as long as you tell me everything you know about Emily. Sound good?"

"Uh... Yeah. Cool."

Preston stood, waited for Cameron to join him.

Wes turned in his seat to look at them. "Bro, the gala hasn't even started."

Preston patted him on the shoulder. "Take good notes during the Powerpuff presentation."

He flung his arm around Cameron again and directed him toward the doors. "I want to hear it all. What she likes, what she hates. Is she a Cubs fan or a Sox fan? When did she lose her virginity? Don't leave anything out, especially when it comes to the details of her virginity."

The trap was set. Cameron had proven useful. Not only had he gotten Preston some face-to-face time with Emily after the gala, but Cameron had built him up enough that she'd agreed to have dinner with him.

They'd had an exquisite meal—and many exquisite drinks—at Alinea. It relaxed her some. Enough that she'd agreed to more drinks at his place. It would be there, high above the city in his sixtieth-floor apartment, that Emily would release any anxieties she had left and tell him everything he needed to know. And once that was out of the way, maybe he'd take her onto the balcony where she could enjoy a great view and a great fuck.

Her eyes widened as the limo pulled up to his building. "You live here?"

"Yes. One of the penthouses."

A wide smile slid across her face. "When I was little, I loved buildings like these. Whenever we'd come to the Loop for dinner or something, on the way in, I'd pretend that I lived in one of these high rises and that my driver was taking me home after some important meeting in the western 'burbs." She laughed a tipsy laugh. "I have no idea what important business anyone would have in the 'burbs, but I was a kid."

He glanced at her cleavage, loosely shrouded by the shiny fabric of her black spaghetti-strap dress. "You are definitely no longer a kid."

She sat up, covered her tits with her left palm. "Shut up, perv." Her right hand landed a playful slap on his arm and lingered before sliding down to the bend in his elbow.

Maybe the limo was overkill, but tonight was about selling a dream. Showing her all that was possible if she allied herself with the right people. He didn't have to be a predator. She didn't have to be a victim. There was room for both of them to win. If she were to follow his advice, she could live the kind of life she'd always dreamed of.

The door opened and Preston slid out, offered his hand to Emily. Sliding her hand under the fabric of her dress, she cupped it close to her legs as she slid out, her strappy high heels settling on the pavement beneath her. She pulled on his arm until her feet were set, then wandered across the sidewalk and gazed up at the building. She was hooked. He had her. The limo, the fancy dinner, and his apartment all had worked together to ensnare her. She was now his to do with what he pleased.

Preston turned to the driver, smirked. "I won't be needing the car again this evening."

He opened the door and allowed her to walk in first. After a few steps, the shimmering city below lit up her face.

"Holy shit!" She stepped toward the windows in the main living room. "You've got views on all sides."

"City, river, and lake. I've got two private patios as well. One has an amazing lake view, the other faces south. Unobstructed views of all of downtown."

She wandered from one window to the next with the wonderment of a child stepping into an FAO Schwarz store.

Leaving her to fall deeper into the trap, Preston opened a bottle of wine and poured them each a glass. He set the glasses on the table in front of the sofa, then took a seat, allowing her to get comfortable with her surroundings, and for what was next.

Emily was special. Sexy, smart. She could be useful in a number of ways. He could easily get the intel he needed to take her company, but doing that would certainly end their relationship on an unpleasant note. If instead he convinced her to dump her business partner, perhaps merge her company into Carter & Nichols' portfolio, he might find a place for her. Certainly as an occasional plaything, but also within the company.

She clearly possessed what it took to make it in his world and knew how to get what she wanted. Her dress proved that she was cunning, that she was comfortable using any asset available to her. Silky and form-fitting, it hugged her hips and teased with hints of what her body would look like once he got the dress off her. The strategically placed slit up the left side tempted, offering brief glimpses of her smooth leg. The bustier top cupped her round tits and showed just enough that he was left wanting more.

Once she'd had her fill of the views, she joined him. He handed her a glass of wine and she sat beside him, tucking her dress beneath her as she collapsed onto the sofa.

"This place is gorgeous." She sipped from the glass.

"It's one of my many homes. Perhaps I can show you the others someday soon."

Her eyes widened. "Where else do you have homes?"

"I've got a similar apartment in New York, a beach house in Palm Beach, and a magnificent condo in Aspen that's just steps from the lifts."

"Wow. I can't even imagine living this way. You're very lucky."

He held up his glass. "To capitalism. It's been good to me."

She clinked her glass against his. "This apartment is everything I'd want in a place to live. Hopefully I'll have something like it someday."

"I think you will. You have what it takes. I can see it in you."

She blushed. "Well, thank you. Let's hope so. I could get used to living in a place like this."

Placing his arm on the back of the sofa behind her, he turned to examine his apartment. "It's come a long way. When I bought it, it was a mess. But I got a good deal, and then I did a two-million-dollar renovation to get it to where it is now."

"Holy shit!" She choked on the wine she was swallowing. "Two million? Well, it looks incredible."

"Thank you." With his fingers, he pushed her bangs from her eyes and studied her youthful face. "One of my strengths is recognizing undervalued assets and then investing in them."

"Well, you've done an amazing job here."

"Thanks, but I think you know I'm talking about you."

She blushed again, looked away from him. "That's sweet of you to say."

"I mean it. You've got what it takes to have all of this. You just need the right tools."

She chuckled. "Tools? Like access to a few million dollars?"

"It may sound like a lot now, but you'll get there in no time."

A tight smile crept across her face. "I don't know about that. Seems the better Blossom Ridge does, the more of my money goes straight to taxes."

"That's an easy problem to solve."

Her eyes narrowed. "How?"

"The Caribbean." He chuckled. "The Cayman Islands are your best friend."

"Seriously? I mean, I've always heard that, but are you telling me that it's actually possible to avoid taxes there?"

He smiled. He had her on the hook, but he had to be careful reeling her in. "It's completely true."

"How does that work though? You just fly down there, walk into a bank and say, 'I'm an American and I want one of those secret, tax-free bank accounts I'm always hearing about.'"

He smiled, a genuine smile. She was as funny as she was sexy. "Something like that, yeah."

"I'm asking seriously. How the hell do you set something like that up?"

"You get a guy."

"So? You've got a guy?"

He nodded. "His name's Robert."

"So Robert handles all of that stuff for you?"

"He set me up with these foreign trusts, along with some private equity funds—a series of limited partnerships and LLCs. And then he filters money through the trusts. I don't really know how all of it works, but I do know that it keeps me from pissing away a fortune."

"Awesome." She sipped her wine. "So how'd you find this guy?"

"I met him through my dad. He'd set him up with some similar things in Bermuda way back in the day."

"Think he can set that up for me?"

"I'm not sure he's seeking new clients these days. But we can find you a guy. Someone who offers asset protection planning, that's what you're looking for."

Her eyes narrowed. "I don't know. Bermuda. The Caymans. Isn't that stuff illegal?"

He brushed her hair aside again, stroked her cheek with the back of his fingers. "Legality is subjective. If the government ever finds out, they'll just make me pay some fines. Money makes anything legal." He chuckled. "Like they say, if something is labeled 'punishable by a fine,' all that means is that it's legal for a fee."

She smiled at that, and he leaned in, kissed her wine-coated lips. He was about to slide closer, explore her body with his hands, but she turned away from the embrace.

"You know, Miranda didn't want me to go out with you."

Christ. This was going to require more work than he'd thought. He released a sharp breath. "No? Why not? She want me all to herself?"

Emily smirked. "I think it had to do more with some stuff she read about you. Something about you being a corporate spy who uses what he learns to force troubled companies into more trouble."

"The media is so dramatic." He rolled his eyes. "All I do is seek out distressed companies that have good intellectual property, and then I buy them on a down tick. I make my money back by licensing that valuable IP to other companies that need it. It's a win-win. They get what they need to grow, and I make money from the licensing."

"Still, some say tomato..."

He laughed at the cute face she made as she let the phrase dangle in the air between them. "It's not as sinister as the media makes it out to be. It's exhilarating, actually. The hunt. Striking when they don't see it coming. It's better than the best sex you've ever had."

She smiled. "Well, when you put it that way."

She was back on the hook, tantalized. She had everything needed to thrive in his world. She could be ruthless, and she wanted to be. It was written all over her face. The good girl act was just that: an act. She wanted to be bad. To take things, not make them.

He slid his hand onto her thigh, under the slit in her dress, and onto her bare leg. "You've got what it takes, you know?"

"What it takes to do what?"

"To live like this." He waved his free hand toward the view outside the window. "You can accomplish this, and you don't need people like Miranda to do it."

"Miranda's my best friend."

"I'm not saying she can't be your friend. What I'm saying is that I can see that she's the one holding you back. Holding back the success of your company."

"No." Her body tensed. "That's not it at all. Miranda's great."

"I'm sure she's a great person, but I'm talking about her as a business partner. There's got to be something about her that you think is impeding bigger successes."

"I couldn't ask for a better partner." She shifted her weight on the sofa, fidgeted with her wine glass. She was uncomfortable because she was lying.

"C'mon." He removed his hand from her leg, brushed the hair from her face with his fingers. "I can see there's something that bothers you."

She exhaled sharply. "Well, I mean... Sorta."

"I knew it." He smiled. "What is it?"

She released a long, deep breath. "Well, okay. Sometimes she'll make changes to code, like, out of nowhere she'll have some new idea, and she'll implement it without running it by anyone else. Sometimes it works out, but sometimes she wrecks things, and it takes us a day or two to get back to where we were."

"See. I knew there was something."

"So what? Just because of that I should get rid of her? Pull a Zuckerberg? Issue a bunch of new shares and dilute her ownership?"

He laughed. "So you've thought about it?" He leaned over, grabbed the wine bottle from the table, and refilled her glass.

"No, I haven't. I've just seen *The Social Network* too many times." She sipped from the glass. "To be clear: I've never thought of pushing her out of the company."

"You want this though, right? The views? The exquisite meals and expensive wines? You can have all of this." He took the glass from her hand, set it on the table. Leaning in, he kissed her lips, allowed his hand to slide up the slit in her dress, higher this time, to her hip.

She leaned away, then stood. "I, um... I should go. I have an early day tomorrow."

"On a Sunday? You a priest or something?"

She grabbed her clutch and stepped around the table. "Thank you for dinner. That was a lovely restaurant."

He stepped to the other side of the table to block her exit. She had nowhere to go. They were sixty floors above Chicago, and he'd sent the limo away.

Preston grabbed her by the arm, kissed her. His other hand on her thigh, he slid it under her dress, grabbed at her panties.

She jerked away, shoved him with both hands, then thrust her foot into his crotch.

The pain dropped him to one knee.

Feeling as though he may vomit, he scurried to his feet as she opened the front door and grabbed her arm.

She turned toward him, shoved him again, struck him between the eyes with her elbow on the bridge of his nose. His vision blurred; he leaned on the table by the door to ward off the dizziness.

She probably thought she'd gotten away, but the elevator wouldn't be there for at least a few minutes. With blood dripping from his nose, he flung the door open, charged into the hallway. "You stupid bitch!"

She stood waiting for the elevator, but she wasn't alone. Several neighbors had stepped into the hallway, and one was standing near Emily, blocking his path to her.

He backed into the doorway. "Get the fuck out of here."

He slammed the door shut.

It'd been days since Emily stormed out of his apartment and nothing had come of it, but Wes was terrified that she would file charges, that she'd claim he raped her or something.

Wes sat down on the edge of Preston's desk. "Look, bro, all I'm saying is that we need to get ahead of this shit. We've got to find something to discredit her."

"Fine. Get Cameron in here. He knows her. He can point us in the right direction."

"He's not in today."

"What? Where the fuck is he?"

"I dunno. He called in sick."

"Well, get him on the phone. Have him find us as many guys as he can who knew her in high school or college. Guys who fucked her. Guys who wanted to fuck her. Guys who went on dates with her. Anyone willing to discuss what a fucking slut she is."

"You got it." Wes stood. "What's the plan? Destroy her credibility before she talks?"

Preston shook his head. "We're going to have to make her a deal. Cut her a check to keep her mouth shut but let her know that if she doesn't keep it shut, we'll destroy her publicly with every detail of her sex life."

"Is that a big enough threat?"

"It'd crush her personally, and since she's the face of Blossom Ridge, it would also wreck their shitty little company. Faced with those realities, she'll uphold the deal."

Wes didn't respond. His attention shifted to the doorway, shifted to the area outside Preston's office where the sound of office chatter rose, then quieted.

Wes strolled out the door. Preston followed to find several men in cheap suits coming his way. Detectives, he figured. The bitch did it. She'd gone to the cops and claimed he tried to rape her.

But that wasn't it. They flashed IDs. They weren't local cops. They were federal agents. It was all a blur, too many people chattering at once for him to focus. He heard only parts of sentences.

"Indicted."

"Violations of the Internal Revenue Code."

"Violations of U.S. Code."

"Title Twenty Six."

"Title Thirty One."

She'd gotten him. She must have been wired. That's what the whole night had been about. And Cameron—that fucking weasel. Did he even know her, or was he planted by the feds?

Outside the building, a couple of reporters gathered, no doubt alerted to FBI activity at the headquarters of Carter & Nichols. A woman from Channel 2 shouted questions, but Preston couldn't hear what she'd asked, even if he wanted to respond.

He stepped off the curb and looked back at the building. Some staff members had followed them to the ground floor and gathered by the fountain. Some bystanders had stopped to watch too. And then, his eyes shifted to them: Emily and Miranda, watching as the agents led him to the awaiting car. Delighting in his arrest. At least the smile on Emily's face proved he was right about her. She definitely knew how to get what she wanted.

THE ROAD OUT

The parking lot was empty. Only three letters in the old neon vacancy sign still flickered. At a glance, it seemed the Bestvalu Motor Inn had been abandoned years ago, but as I drove up to the office, I spotted a woman seated at a desk behind a sheet of bulletproof glass.

The motel was a fleabag, that was apparent even in the dark of night, but it looked like the kind of place where I could get a room without creating a paper trail of my stay, so I got out of my truck and approached the woman.

She spoke few words and wore no expression as she confirmed she had a room available.

I smiled and said, "Sounds good. I'll take it."

"I'll need your driver's license."

With a quick pat of my pockets, I pretended to search for my wallet. "Oh, shoot. My apologies, ma'am, but I think I might have left my wallet at the gas station back there."

She stared without muttering a word.

Resting a forearm on the metal shelf in front of the glass, I said, "If there's a way we can do this without my ID, it'd be much appreciated. I'll call the gas station and get them to hold onto my wallet, but I've been driving all night, and I really need some rest."

She stared, then said, "Can't rent a room without ID. That's policy."

With a nod, I again pretended to search my jean pockets and even emptied a few items onto the metal counter for effect—a lighter, my keys. I patted my shirt pockets, then reached under the flap of one and pulled out a fifty and a one-hundred-dollar bill. I placed them casually on the counter next to my keys, then nudged the bills slightly until they slid into the indentation under the glass. "You sure there's not some other way?"

She glanced at Mr. Franklin and his pal Mr. Grant, then returned her gaze to me. In a quick motion, her hand swept up the bills. "I guess I can let it slide this one time."

"Thank you, ma'am. I sure do appreciate you. I'll go get my wallet after I get some sleep."

"Mmm-hmm." She pushed a few buttons on a keyboard, then slid a key under the glass. "Room twenty four. On the end, by the vending machines."

I moved my truck to the other side of the empty lot, parked near the dumpsters, and collected the few things I had with me. I flung my backpack over a shoulder, then slid the pistol-grip Mossberg shotgun between it and my back, out of sight. I untucked my shirt and concealed the Glock pistol in my waistband, draped the duffle over my other shoulder, and lumbered toward room twenty four.

A musty smell greeted me when I opened the door. I dropped the duffle onto the worn carpet below, then fumbled for the light switch. A single bedside lamp illuminated the dreary room, showcasing its nicotine-stained walls and tattered bedding that hadn't been updated in decades, much like the tiny town outside the door. It was easy to envision a time when the Bestvalu and the town were vibrant places—back before Eisenhower built interstate highways that allowed drivers to bypass places like it.

I'd purposely avoided those modern interstate high-ways though, sticking instead to back roads that wound through lightly traveled towns. One of those roads led me to a bright blue sign that screamed: WELCOME TO VAUGHN, CROSSROADS OF NEW MEXICO. A little bit past the sign sat the Bestvalu, the first motel I'd seen after hours of driving.

I locked the door and drew the curtains shut. Sitting at the small table in the corner, I began dismantling the Mossberg. The barrel came off easily enough but freeing the trigger assembly proved to be a bit trickier. Best I could tell, one small pin held everything in place, so I freed my Leatherman from the sheath clipped to my belt and extended the punch tool. With a bit of force, I managed to push the pin out of place, and after that, the rest of the gun came apart without issue.

Pulling the curtain aside, I peered across the parking lot. Confident I was alone, I gathered the smallest pieces of the shotgun and took them to the dumpster on the edge of the lot. Tomorrow, after I'd gotten some sleep, I'd get rid of the bigger parts, scattering them in a few different places to prevent someone from ever finding the entire gun. Without the gun, the cops couldn't prove shit.

The headlights pierced the tattered curtains, setting the room aglow with diffused light. Sliding from the bed to the floor, I crawled to the window with the Glock in my hand.

Wedged in the corner of the room, I nudged the curtain away from the wall with the barrel of the gun and peered out toward the parking lot. The lights shut off, returning the room to darkness. The scarce lights in the lot backlit two figures—one tall, one stocky.

After exhaling a long, steady breath to calm my nerves, I again peered out the window, my finger poised on the trigger guard. The tall one stood just a couple feet from the door to my room; the stocky one stood near the vehicle.

Using my free hand, I wiped my eyes clean. I'd only gotten a couple hours of sleep, at best. No one had come or gone from the place since I'd arrived, so these two had to be looking for me. They likely knew Adan, although I had no idea what any of his associates looked like. Hell, I'd never met Adan until last night—a meeting that, to say the least, left a bad taste in my mouth.

Forcing myself to inhale long, even breaths, I allowed my eyes to close for a moment. It helped to steady my nerves, but adrenaline continued to flow, and my muscles tightened. Again, I leaned toward the window and peered through the curtains. The tall one moved away from the door and walked toward the back of the vehicle. I released another long breath and moved my finger to the trigger, ready to defend myself.

The stocky one stepped off the sidewalk and walked to the other side of the vehicle. The back door opened, and a small child slid out of the back seat.

Releasing all the air in my lungs, I loosened my grip on the Glock. It was just a family stopping at a motel for the night, not someone sent to kill me.

I leaned against the heater below the window, pushed myself to my feet, and headed toward the sink where I set the pistol on the cracked vanity and flipped on the cold faucet. The face in the mirror didn't look like me at all, and not in a cheesy sense like *I can't believe who I've become*, rather, I looked tired. I looked defeated. I looked like someone in some deep shit with no plan to get out of it, which was exactly the case.

If anyone asked, room twenty four was currently rented to Paul Anderson, a name I created on the spot during check in, and as far as I knew, no one was looking for Paul Anderson.

Unfortunately, in the parking lot sat a Ram truck registered in my real name, and lots of people were looking for me. I was sure of that because, a couple hundred miles east in a shitty part of Amarillo, someone had ransacked my apartment. Most likely Adan's guys, but it also could have been the cops. Even if it wasn't the cops, I figured that, by now, they'd visited the home of Cole, my best friend, and there they surely found four dead bodies.

I needed a plan. When the sun came up, my red truck would draw attention like a neon sign in the dark of night, just like the sign outside the Bestvalu had grabbed my attention. Once someone spotted that truck, they'd find me here, holed up in a tiny room with a dismantled Mossberg Maverick 88 and a Glock 21 with just thirteen rounds in the magazine. Not a lot of ammo for dealing with the kinds of enemies I'd made.

She smiled as she set my food in front of me, a large platter with a heaping pile of hash browns and two of everything else: bacon, sausage links, and eggs. She set down a second plate with two pancakes stacked on it. "Can I get ya anything else?"

I shook my head. "No, thank you, ma'am. This'll do nicely."

She placed the check down beside the coffee mug. "No rush on this."

It was early and the diner was busy, probably because it was about the only place in town to eat—a classic retro joint that appealed to people nostalgic for a simpler time. I'd been there for about forty minutes, pounding coffee and listening to the cacophony of forks scraping against plates as I tried to force my sleep-deprived brain to formulate some kind of plan.

"Refill?"

I looked up to see a coffeepot hovering above my cup. "Please."

My eyes met hers as she poured.

Again she smiled.

Mia, her nametag read. Short and curvy with glowing brown eyes and a long brown ponytail that whipped around behind her as she moved. I supposed she was a few years younger than me, maybe twenty one or twenty two.

Mia rested the coffeepot on her palm. "How is everything tasting?"

"It's all delicious, thank you."

"Those hash browns cooked enough for ya?"

"Yes, ma'am. They're very good. Lots of butter."

"I like 'em well done." She chuckled. "Burnt, as my mom calls it."

I smiled and offered a chuckle. "I guess I prefer them this way. Crispy on top, but soft underneath."

A man at another table interrupted our conversation. "Excuse me!" His tone was obnoxious and condescending.

Mia sighed. "Well, please let me know if I can get ya anything else."

"Thank you," I said with another smile as she turned her attention to the douchebag.

He clearly wasn't a local because, while all the men in the diner wore the unofficial uniform of the rural West—jeans, boots, and button-down shirts—Mr. Douchebag looked like he was about to go golfing: mint green polo shirt, khaki shorts, and Velcro sandals. He'd been annoying since his arrival when he blew past the sign that requested patrons to wait to be seated, then commandeered a table at the back, in a section that the diner obviously didn't have staffed.

Douchebag flailed his hands wildly as he yelled at Mia about the quality of the breakfast burrito he'd ordered, which apparently was not made the same way as the burritos he usually ordered in whatever pretentious big city he'd rolled in from.

I shifted my gaze to the window and stared out at the small town. I hated to leave, but I had to because the place was located about three and a half hours from Amarillo, and that was just too close. I needed more separation between me and my problems. Even if it wasn't the cops who tossed my apartment, I was certain that they'd gotten a warrant by now. Cole's place had probably been picked apart last night, and homicide detectives were likely still questioning neighbors.

We never should have gotten hooked up with Adan. I never wanted to do business with him in the first place, but Cole ignored my warnings. The simple fact was that we didn't need Adan. Shit was going just fine. We had a good business going, selling weed to college kids and meat packers. I was never looking to expand, and I sure as hell never wanted to get mixed up with shit like fentanyl.

I don't think Cole was looking for that either, but Adan didn't give us a choice. He kept forcing more product on us—stuff our customers didn't want—and yet, Adan expected us to have money for him each week, no exceptions.

I took a sip of coffee, then patted the backpack at my feet, something I'd been doing all morning—a way to confirm it was still there. It was all I had at this point: seventy grand, minus the four hundred or so I'd spent in the past thirteen hours. A mind-blowing amount of cash. Far more than I'd ever had on me at one time. Frankly, I'd never expected to hold this kind of cash in my life, and I wouldn't be holding it if Adan had just given us our fair cut of it in the first place. He'd also be alive right now, and so would Cole.

Adan's side of things, if you were able to speak to ghosts, would be that Cole got greedy by demanding to keep an extra five grand from our recent sales, and that

Cole brought all of this down on us when he decided to hang onto the full seventy grand to make a point. But now, Cole, Adan, and his two thugs were dead, and I had a bag full of cash at my feet.

"Another refill?" Mia's lovely voice startled me from my reverie.

I offered her a smile and said, "No, thank you. I've gotta run soon."

"If you're sure." She smiled back at me and said, "I can pour it in a to-go cup if ya'd like?"

"Thank you. That'd be great."

She turned swiftly and walked toward the counter.

I finished the coffee in the mug and stared at my empty plate, my mind wandering, imagining how things would be if Cole hadn't pushed Adan. I understood why he had, and I agreed that we deserved the extra five grand for all the trouble Adan had caused us, but still, I wished it had all played out differently. Presumably, Cole was afraid of Adan but wanted to act like he wasn't. The guy claimed to have ties to a Texas prison gang, and he'd made plenty of threats about his associates finding Cole and killing him. Maybe it was all bullshit. Maybe not. If it *was* true, then I imagined his gang associates were now looking for me, and the seventy grand at my feet.

"Here ya go." Mia set a Styrofoam cup on the table. "I was going to see if ya needed a box, but it looks like you tackled all of that pretty well."

"Yes, ma'am. Guess I was hungry."

"Well, if I can get ya anything else, just holler."

Douchebag again demanded her attention.

Mia saw me watching him and said, "We've already remade his entire meal, to his exact specifications. Who knows what's wrong now?"

"Perhaps his diaper is full?"

She chuckled, a sound of genuine amusement. "Maybe. Guess I'll go find out. Do let me know if ya need anything else though, and come see me again soon, 'k?"

"I surely will. Thank you for everything, Mia."

"You bet." She turned on her heels and walked toward Douchebag.

I took a gander at the check. Under fifteen bucks for all that food and all that coffee. Not bad at all. I pulled out a fifty, set it on top of the check, and slid both under the edge of the plate. Douchebag sure wasn't gonna tip well, so I hoped it helped.

While Mia dealt with the asshole in the mint green polo, I hoisted the backpack onto my shoulder and slipped out the front door. Feeling full and refreshed, I was ready to take care of some of the problems in my way. For starters, there was my truck. By now cops had surely put my plate number into several databases, so I needed to ditch the plates. I needed to blend in. To look like any other New Mexican driving through the Land of Enchantment.

I freed my cigarettes from my shirt pocket, lit one, then strolled to the side of the building. Plopping the backpack down beside me, I knelt behind a silver BMW and set the coffee cup down on the pavement. I pretended to adjust my pant leg over my boot, then unsheathed my Leatherman and extended the Phillips bit.

The plate came off the sedan easily. It was brand new and so were the threads on the screws. Rising to my feet, I looked around to make sure I hadn't attracted any attention. With the yellow license plate tucked under my arm, I picked up my coffee and leaned against the building to finish my cigarette.

Southbound US 285 offered a barren landscape where the first forty miles were indistinguishable from the next forty, at least until I neared Roswell where the billboards hawking alien attractions began.

Choosing to skip the infamous town and its extraterrestrial attractions, I took a truck route that looped me around the traffic through town but offered even less to look at than the main road. I hoped that fewer cops patrolled the bypass, even if I did drive with the mindset of a local now that the yellow New Mexico plate hung from the bumper of my truck. It hit me then though that I would need to get rid of my truck. I'd miss her, but I had no choice.

One question that'd been on my mind was if I would have been better off taking Cole's truck instead. But Cole was dead, and in many ways, a dead man's truck stood out more.

Problem was, I didn't have a whole lot of time to think about things like that last night. I'd been taking a piss when Adan and his thugs pushed their way through Cole's front door. I heard the commotion and hurried out of the bathroom in time to see Adan hitting Cole with a red and blue Texas Rangers Louisville Slugger as he shouted about the cash Cole had been withholding, and about how we didn't appreciate all that he did for us.

What *he* did for us? It still made me laugh. All he did was load us up with a bunch of product we couldn't move quickly enough, and when we did manage to sell it, he forced us to move even more.

At any rate, shit got out of hand fast and when I heard the shouting, I hid in Cole's bedroom. Sure, it was a pussy move, but damn it, I didn't know what else to do.

From the relative safety of the bedroom, I watched as the two big guys punched Cole until he fell to his knees, and then they held his arms while Adan rammed the fat end of the Louisville Slugger into his face. I heard his nose break on the first shot. I can still hear it if I think about it too much.

"Where's my money, bitch?" Adan shouted.

Cole refused to tell him where the cash was, so Adan jabbed Cole in the jaw, loosening some of his teeth, which he later spit across the room.

Adan shouted again, his face inches from Cole's. "Where's the money?"

Cole didn't answer, I think because he was almost unconscious.

Adan then swung the bat at Cole's ribs. I heard the crack, and I'm sure it broke some of them.

Adan leaned the bat against the wall, pulled a Glock out of his waistband, shoved the barrel in Cole's face, and shouted, "I'm only gonna ask you one more time. Where's my money?"

Cole whimpered like an abused dog but didn't speak. I supposed he was acting tough, though I didn't know why. Perhaps he thought there was some possible way that he'd survive the ordeal, and maybe he hoped that people would hear that he'd stood up to Adan.

Adan wasn't going to let Cole be a hero though. He racked the slide and returned the gun to Cole's face. "Last chance, bitch. Where's my money?"

Cole whimpered as he nodded his chin toward the coat closet by the front door.

Adan returned the Glock to his waistband and began tossing items from the closet. When he found the backpack, he unzipped it and peered inside. Satisfied that all the cash was back in his possession, Adan picked up the bat and laughed—a disturbing noise that still reverberated in my head and kept me awake last night.

With a grin on his face, he took a full swing at Cole's head.

The two big guys let go of Cole as the bat came their way. It connected with Cole's skull and made a sound that

I'll never forget. It seemed to linger, like when a firework exploded, and the noise floated in the air for miles.

Most likely the blow killed Cole, but that piece of shit kept swinging the bat, even after Cole's lifeless body fell to the ground.

Cole always kept a loaded Mossberg shotgun by his bedside, and as anger and fear washed over me, I grabbed it, pumped it, and charged toward the living room.

From the hallway, I fired a blast. Pumped. Fired. Pumped. Fired.

The first blast hit one of the big guys in the chest and he went down quickly. The second blast struck Adan and dropped him. The other big guy turned and ran out the front door. I pumped, followed, and fired.

He dropped to the ground, and when I caught up to him, I stood over him, pumped, and fired again.

Once the shock of it all settled, I ran back inside to check on Cole, but I could tell he was dead before I even knelt beside him. My ears rung and everything else sounded muffled. I didn't know what to do, but I knew I didn't want to be there when the cops showed up. I also knew that after that many shotgun blasts in a residential area, they'd arrive soon.

Some kind of instinctive autopilot took over my limbs and used them to grab the Glock from Adan's waistband, then the Mossberg, and then the backpack.

I hurried to my truck and raced to my place, nearly hyperventilating as I drove. It was a short drive, but the reality of things had set in by the time I got home. It seemed like my apartment would be a safe space to regroup, but when I arrived, I found the front door wide open.

Glock in hand, I cleared my apartment. Whoever had been there was gone, but they'd trashed the place, probably while searching for the cash. My autopiloted brain told me

I had to get out of there, and out of Amarillo, so I stuffed some clothing and a few important items into a duffle and hit the road.

Lost in thought, I almost failed to notice that the speed limit dropped as I passed a sign announcing my arrival in the town of Carlsbad. Avoiding a very costly mistake, I lifted my foot off the accelerator and slowed to below the new limit. The yellow plate on my bumper might have made me look like any other New Mexican on my way to popular attractions like the Carlsbad Caverns, but the last goddamned thing I needed was for some cop to run that plate, because it sure as hell wasn't registered to the 2001 Ram Club Cab it was affixed to.

Sticking to the main road, I took a drive through town to check things out a bit. The place looked like a regular ol' town—a good place for any search for me to come to an end.

With the window down, I took in some fresh air and peered out at the Pecos River as it curved along the road. Before long, I came to a truck stop.

Using my turn signal and obeying all traffic laws, I pulled into the parking lot and looked around. The place seemed busy, with both commercial trucks and everyday people stopping for fuel and food. I made a mental note of the location before I headed back toward the north end of town.

I pulled off onto a farm road and drove away from town, stopping briefly to switch into four-wheel drive when the road became washed out near the river's edge. When I came to a clearing, I pulled over near a small ravine along the river and hopped out. Reaching behind the driver's seat, I grabbed my duffle and hoisted it onto the hood of the truck, then dug through it until I located a pair of boxers, which I set aside. I rearranged the remaining clothes to make room for the backpack. It took some doing and I had to ditch some of my clothing in the back of the truck, but I managed to make the backpack fit inside the duffle and even get it zipped shut. I slid the Glock into one of the outside pockets, a convenient spot where it wasn't noticeable but was still accessible if I needed it.

Grabbing my Leatherman from my belt, I pulled out the Phillips bit and freed the yellow plate from my bumper. It'd served me well, but it seemed best that no one knew I ever had it.

I took the plate, and the Mossberg's receiver, and walked over to the riverbank. The receiver was the last piece of the shotgun. I'd ditched the grip and barrel back in the desert along 285 when I stopped to pee.

I flung the license plate toward the river, letting it soar through the air like a frisbee. After catching the breeze for a moment, it drifted into the Pecos with an unimpressive splash. The receiver made a bigger splash but disappeared without ceremony.

Returning to my truck, I took all the documents out of the glove box and shoved them in the other side pocket of my duffle. No doubt someone would find my truck in the next few days, but there was no good reason to make identifying its owner easy for them.

Secure in the idea that nothing with my personal information remained in the cab, I stopped and stared at the truck. It held lots of memories. I'd purchased it back when I started working on the loading docks—the same place I met Cole. I started there just a few weeks after moving to Amarillo, and I bought the truck about two months later. It wasn't in great shape and came with plenty of dents, and while the guys at work had strong opinions on why I should buy a Chevy or a Ford, the Ram was what I could afford at the time. I'd always planned to trade it in someday—exchange it for something fancier that told people I was a success. But not long after I became successful, Cole met Adan and fucked up all of my plans.

I unbuttoned my left sleeve, rolled the material back, grabbed my Leatherman, and extended the main blade. I closed my eyes and readied myself for the pain. It would hurt, I was certain of that, but probably not for long.

With one more sharp exhale, I opened my eyes, pressed the blade against my flesh, then jerked it in one quick motion.

The initial sting was intense but manageable. Using two fingers, I pulled on the wound and allowed blood to pool. With my right hand, I wiped some of it on the steering wheel, then let the wound drip on the upholstery before smashing it in with my palm.

Content with the authenticity of the crime scene I'd manufactured, I grabbed my water bottle and irrigated the wound. Once the bleeding subsided, I used the Leatherman to cut a piece of cloth from a pair of boxers to bandage myself with, then rolled my shirt sleeve back in place, covering the makeshift bandage.

Once authorities located my truck, a glance at the blood stains would hopefully lead them to believe I was dead—perhaps believe that Adan's prison gang friends had found me before they had. People rarely spent time looking for dead men.

It was a two-mile walk to the truck stop, an easy trek for anyone not carrying a bag full of cash. About a mile in, my left shoulder throbbed, so I stopped and switched the bag to my other side. I estimated I'd be at the truck stop in about thirty minutes, and then my shoulders could rest.

As I turned the corner onto the main drag, my heart pounded at the sight of flashing lights from a cop car.

It was all over.

My stomach tightened and I dropped the bag. I could run, but for how long? They likely had dogs and maybe a helicopter. They might even enlist help from border patrol. And if I ran, I'd have to leave the money behind. What was the point of freedom if you had no money?

Running wasn't an option. Instead, I'd take a stand, deny everything, and try to come up with a plausible story about the cash. With a lot of luck, I'd get to keep it.

Exhaling a deep breath, I turned to face the cops.

They hadn't come for me though. The officer had pulled someone over. Some douchebag driving a silver BMW. Apparently, cops here didn't like it when people drove through their town without a license plate on their car.

Douchebag, still wearing his mint green polo, flailed his arms wildly as he pleaded his case to the cop, a thick man with broad shoulders who didn't seem to buy the story about why his fancy new car didn't have a plate.

I hoisted the duffle back onto my shoulder and continued toward the truck stop. I figured it would take me a little while to find someone headed north who'd be willing to let me tag along, but if I could at least get to Colorado tonight, I'd be in good shape. My truck likely wouldn't be found for a day or two, and even if they didn't believe I was dead, after finding my truck so far south, they'd probably think I fled to Mexico. Having search efforts focused on the southern border would give me time to get to Montana where my cousin would let me crash at his place for as long as I needed. He'd probably make me help out on the ranch, but that'd be okay. I didn't mind hard work

ACKNOWLEDGMENTS

I would like to thank my good friend Kat Glover who read early drafts of about half of the stories in this collection and whose feedback and honesty helped make them better.

Many thanks to my parents Greg and Sandi Lowery and to my grandfather Robert Thornton for many years of encouragement and for always supporting my writing endeavors.

Thanks to all my Illinois family who've always made the state feel like home, especially my great-aunt Galena Lowery and my grandfather Keith Lowery, who I still miss dearly.

Last but most, my wife Aimee Lowery. She's the best first reader and her editing makes me a better writer, but her constant love and support makes me a better human.

ABOUT THE AUTHOR

R.M. Lowery is the award-winning author of the Jakob Larsen Mysteries—*The Gentle Slope*, *We Kill Our Own*, and *Time Fades Away*, along with the novels *Laytons Grove* and *What Was Left*. His short fiction has appeared in *Black Cat Mystery Magazine*, *Workers Write*, *The First Line*, and others. Lowery lives in Colorado with his beautiful wife and their clowder (of cats).